AMBUSH!

"Shoot!" Linus Derks squalled and ran back a few steps.

Owen rolled after he hit the street. A bullet plocked into the street beside his head, kicking snow into his face. He snapped a shot at the dark figure on Alderson's roof and heard the shrill, following scream.

Something heavy and hot tore through Owen's coat and burned across his shoulder. That shot came from the other side of the street and he flung himself about.

He caught a glimpse of movement and fired three rapid shots. The shadowy bulk disappeared, and he was sure he heard frantic steps retreating across the roof.

He flopped over to face Derks, stopping short when he finally saw him.

Derks had a gun in his hand, a gun aimed at Enoch....

Books by Giles A. Lutz

The Bleeding Land
The Hardy Breed
The Long Cold Wind
The Stubborn Breed
The Way Homeward

Published by POCKET BOOKS

THE LONG COLD WIND

Giles Lutz

PUBLISHED BY POCKET BOOKS NEW YORK

POCKET BOOKS, a Simon & Schuster division of
GULF & WESTERN CORPORATION
1230 Avenue of the Americas, New York, N.Y. 10020

Copyright © 1962 by Giles A. Lutz

Published by arrangement with Doubleday & Company, Inc.
Library of Congress Catalog Card Number: 62-13348

ISBN: 0-671-82201-2

First Pocket Books printing October, 1978

Trademarks registered in the United States and other countries.

Printed in the U.S.A.

To Polly:
For Being Polly

THE LONG
COLD WIND

ONE

Montana was never an easy country. It was a land of immensities, a land of savage contrast. Its great, sweeping plains were abruptly halted by jutting mountains, mountains that seemed to reach as far vertically as the plains reached horizontally. It was a silent, brooding land, harshened and roughened under its scourge of weather. Nowhere in its four seasons was ample breathing space, a time to relax, a time to dream. Her winters were hard and wearing, punishing to man and animal. Her summers were hot, the searing winds sucking up the moisture that was the lifeblood to so many things. Spring was a brief, falsely bright season with a lying promise of better things to come that never fully materialized. Fall was as short as spring, an interlude of short, colorful days that delighted the eye. The spirit knew no such delight. Each passing day shriveled the spirit with dread, for close upon the heels of fall trod winter. The weather stropped all forms of life. The soft could not stand the stropping and so perished. The country had only one law, one grim, inexorable law—survive or die.

Two riders traversed a vast plain, making no impression upon its reaches, either with their size or their passing. Both of them watched the ground as they moved, their eyes anxious as though the seeking would restore some great loss. Hoofs crushed the short, yellowing grass, and there was not enough moisture to put resiliency into it. It was only mid-June, and the grass was shorter and yellower than it was ordinarily in late summer.

The older of the two riders said passionately, "It hasn't grown a Goddamned inch the last month."

Owen Parnell nodded agreement to his father's words. A stockman could never live in a day-tight compartment, letting tomorrow take care of itself. Tomorrow carried too many worries. It brought constantly changing conditions—the weather, the shape of the cattle, the possible losses from both two- and four-legged predators. A cattleman never rested securely in the thought that this day was his, for tomorrow could take it all away from him. It took provocation to pull an outbreak like that from Enoch. The short grass was provocation enough. The spring rains had failed, and the summer heat moved in too early. The hot winds and the sun sponged up what little moisture there was in the ground, and the grass started dying. Unless the rains came, it was going to be a long, worrisome summer.

He glanced at the clear sky and the pitiless, brassy sun. Nature was never moderate. She gave too much or too little. A dust devil danced across the plain, and Owen frowned at it. It was a sign of holding, dry weather.

To the right of the riders, Square Butte and the Highwoods loomed up. Due south of them was Judith gap, leading to the Judith mountains. To the left of the gap was the long, snow-capped ridge of the Little Snowies. Far to the northeast, the hazy, blue forms of the Bear Paw mountains rose across the Missouri river.

Forty or fifty head of cattle were gathered at the banks of the clear, cold stream just ahead of them, and Owen followed his father toward them. The cattle moved sluggishly ahead of the riders, their pace telling of their condition. Patches of winter hair still clung to them, giving them a ragged, scruffy appearance. Last winter had been a hard one, and the cattle came through it in poor condition. Without the luxuriant spring grass they built back slowly. These cows were gaunt, their ribs and backbones showing. Owen counted twenty-six calves. The bulk of the calves should have arrived by now, yet this group of cows showed a little better than fifty per cent. Thin cows made for a poor calf crop. The loss would not stop here. It would extend into next year, for a thin cow suckled poorly, and the calves got off to a poor start.

An instant's rebellion twisted his face. A man worked his guts out, building and planning, and nature took it from him. His face straightened. He did not expect his father to comment on the cattle's appearance. It was there for any eye to see.

He let his horse drink. He heard the soft, sucking sound and watched the drops of water fall when the animal raised its muzzle.

The family resemblance was strong between father and son. They were hewn with the same harsh strokes, and only the age discrepancy was apparent. Owen was twenty-four, Enoch in his early sixties. Enoch Parnell married late. The years had already set a stubborn disposition, and no woman's influence could do more than soften its edges. His once black hair was streaked with gray, and his beard stubble showed grizzled against the leather of his skin. His eyebrows were completely white, and the bushy patches made the clear blue of his eyes more startling. They were as piercing as they had ever been, and Owen doubted they would ever dim. Enoch stood six feet, and age's heavy hand had been unable to bend him. His face was craggy, the nose a sharp blade between prominent cheekbones and hollowed cheeks. The lips were thin and severely set. They moved rarely in laughter or jest. His face was an image of the uncompromising nature of the man. He saw things only his way, and there was never another answer.

Owen's face was as lean as his father's, and he stood as tall. His skin had the same weather-roughened appearance, but there was a modification in his features, a modification that came from his mother. His eyes were gray. They could be cold, but humor had the power to warm them. His mouth was bigger than Enoch's, the lips more generous, and laughter was no alien thing to them.

He glanced at his father as Enoch rolled a cigarette. He respected him, but he did not love him. Enoch had no human frailties. He was never wrong, and Owen had never heard him say, "I'm sorry," to anyone. Even after all these years, his father was a cold stranger to him. He knew now there would never be a closeness between them. Since he was old enough to comprehend he had never heard a word of praise from Enoch. But let him do something wrong, and the scathing criticism stripped hide from him. He remembered as a kid how he had yearned for some sign of affection from Enoch. He never received it. It made him a remote man, a careful man. He learned to keep the softer feelings buried deep, where they could not be so easily hurt.

He had something on his mind, something he had been trying all morning to say, and he still looked for the right opening. Once he voiced it, Enoch would explode. Enoch could not stand criticism or opposition.

He rolled his own cigarette, his eyes roaming the country. It was cattle country. The whole country clear to the Yellowstone was good grass country, well watered and well sheltered. An abundance of yellow pine was at the foot of Judith mountains. A man could get all the poles he needed for building and fencing, just for the price of cutting them down. Owen remembered seeing this range for the first time six years ago. Enoch had looked at it, and some kind of rapt shine lighted his face. Owen's eyes had been too dulled with weariness to appreciate it. He had looked at too much land in the past two months. Two months spent on horseback would wear any man—any man but Enoch. They had traveled from twenty to forty miles a day, and Enoch was the first up in the morning and the last to bed at night. He demanded the same discipline from his sons, and Chad was only twelve then. Owen remembered how his brother whimpered at night from sheer weariness, and how fearful he had been that Enoch would hear the boy. They had started from Deer Lodge, and Enoch had demanded his sons be with him. He wanted them to see the range country, he wanted them to learn an appreciation of the best. Montana's future was cattle, and Enoch believed in that future.

It had taken them two months to find the right place, two months of Enoch critically inspecting every mile of the country. Looking back at the search, Owen thought it must have snowed every day, and the nights were bitterly cold. They lived off the country, and he grew sick of the taste of game. There was buffalo for the shooting, and deer and antelope. Each time they came to a new valley, he thought, this is the place we'll stop. But there was always something wrong. This range had too much sage in the grass, that one lacked sufficient winter shelter for the cattle, this one was badly broken up and had no water except in the rivers. The Tongue and the Rosebud rivers had been in flood and difficult to cross. Their banks were steep-cut and their channels deep. The bottoms of the streams were miry, and Enoch passed them by after a glance.

Owen had begun to believe the hunt would never end, when Enoch found this range. Enoch said simply, "This is it," and the long search was over.

Only one other white person was in the country before them. Old man Larkin had a small place on McDonald creek. Enoch spent long hours talking to him. Larkin said there never was deep snow in the winter. It might get as deep as a foot in January, but it didn't stay long. Snows after January were minor, and they couldn't lay because of the sweeping winds. "It's good cattle range," Larkin had said. "Take all of it you want." He made a sweep of his hand at the surrounding country. "It's free."

Enoch had taken what he thought he could hold onto. He laid foundation logs for five claims. None of the land was surveyed, and the only way to hold it was by occupying it. Enoch held it. He held it against the threat of Indians and the threat of greedy men, who saw the same desirability in this land that Enoch did. He smashed every threat as it appeared, and he used his own resources. Four of the original six men he had hired were still with him. The other two were dead. The remaining four grumbled at the old man's orders and cussed him when he was out of hearing. But they stuck with him. They even took a pride in him, saying he was the toughest old bastard this country would ever know.

How they had worked that first summer and winter! The herd had to be driven from Deer Lodge, and buildings had to be constructed. The log stable for the horses came first, a building large enough to accommodate ten horses. The logs were cut at the foot of the Judith mountains and dragged to the building site. The number of them wore a deep path into the sod. The bunkhouse and blacksmith shop formed two sides of the corral. The log house for the family was the last thing built. It was not completed when winter struck, and it was never quite warm enough. Owen cut enough fragrant sweet grass in the meadows to fill the empty bedticks before frost killed the grass. He stuffed them so full that a person's body sank deeply into the Montana feathers. By piling on every available cover, one could sleep warmly enough through the cold winter nights.

The winter of 1880-81 was severe. Old man Larkin said he had never seen anything like it. The cattle were new on the range, and not feeling at home, they drifted badly. Riders were kept busy turning them back at the passes, when they strayed too far. A half dozen horses escaped and returned to their original range.

Chad was only twelve, but he was expected to do a man's work. He did it.

On the fourteenth of January two feet of snow lay on the ground, and the temperature was forty degrees below zero. Owen cursed Larkin for a liar. The family huddled around a glowing stove at night and watched the white line of frost creep farther and farther across the puncheon floors. None of them knew what Enoch was thinking. His eyes had a glittering coldness that matched the frozen snow outside.

Three days later, the flat pancake chinook clouds appeared in the western sky. The wind roared down from the mountains until a man could scarcely stand against it. Snow disappeared as though a torch were held against it, and the gulches and coulees filled with water. Owen learned later how well Enoch had chosen his range. On the other side of the range, in the Judith basin there were three feet of snow on the level. The chinook did not reach the basin, and the snow lay until the first of April.

"I knew I was right," Enoch said softly. He did not know Owen overheard him.

They had a ten per cent winter kill, and Enoch considered the loss nominal.

Owen relived those days as he looked at his father. He recalled the work-filled days that increased in length instead of lessening. For the herd multiplied, and each head meant additional care and work until there weren't enough minutes in a day to do all the things that needed doing. They had three thousand head on their tally books, and Enoch was talking of more cattle.

Owen thought this was the opening he had sought all morning, and he said, "Enoch, you're still not thinking of buying those Texas cattle."

Enoch's eyes turned cold. "I contracted for them the last time I was in Miles City. They'll be here in September."

Another bunch of cows drifted into view, and they moved with the same weakened, shuffling gait. Owen stared at them, then his eyes switched to his father's face. He said, "You want to see more cows come through a winter looking like those?"

The cold in Enoch's eyes deepened. He was meeting opposition. He said, "Shut your damned mouth."

Owen had hold of it, and he could not let it go. "Our last winter kill was thirteen per cent. We've had two bad winters in a row. If we get a dry summer, we won't have enough grass to go into fall, let alone through another winter. And everybody keeps pouring more cattle onto the range."

Enoch should be able to see that. In 1880, the range teemed with buffalo and antelope. Three years later, cattle had pushed them out. Kohrs drove in three thousand head that year. Floweree put three thousand head of Texas cattle on the Sun river range. The Dehart Land and Cattle Company put six thousand cattle on the Rosebud. Every issue of the *Bulletin,* the Miles City newspaper, carried an account of more cattle driven onto the range. By October of '84, it was estimated six hundred thousand head of cattle were eating Montana grass. And that didn't count the horses. The shelter along the streams was not nearly as good. The cattle ate and trompled the brush, and the tall rye grass was disappearing. The tide of cattle continued unchecked the next two years. The profits were fabulous, as much as a hundred per cent, and Eastern money rushed in to pick up some of the easy money.

Enoch's face grew darker. "I know what you're thinking. You never did have the guts to plunge ahead. You never get big by playing it safe. You believe in something, or you don't. I say Montana has enough grass to feed all the cattle in the world."

Owen choked on the ridiculous statement. He started to open his mouth in further argument, and Enoch said, "I told you to shut up."

Owen's mouth closed. This was no different from all the other arguments. He had never won one from Enoch. He saw Enoch rein his horse around and asked, "Where are we going now?"

"I want to see old man Larkin. Maybe I can contract for his hay this year."

Owen followed his father. The last two winters must be worrying Enoch a little, or he would not be seeking additional hay this early. But worry wouldn't be enough to make Enoch take a backward step. He's wrong, Owen thought dully. He felt it with a dread certainty. The dread was like a cold wind blowing down from the mountains, a cold wind in the middle of June.

TWO

Linus Derks stopped his horse and looked at the little cabin on McDonald creek. He made a soundless cackle, showing broken and yellowed teeth.

"Now ain't that a right pretty place, Cully?" He turned his head and looked at his son.

Cully Derks stared at the cabin. It was a tight, weatherproof little structure. It was better than anything they had ever lived in.

"Do you think he'll sell this morning, Pa?"

Linus made the soundless cackle again. "He'll sell. We got us a lever to use against him." He was a squat, powerful-looking man, fat-softened around the edges. His eyes were small and bright, and they were constantly in movement, a sly kind of movement. Linus was fifty years old, and the weathering and the dirt made him look ten years older. His hat was broken at the crown, and a lock of yellow hair poked through the hole. The two-week-old beard was a sandy color against the weather-darkened skin. The skin was loose around his neck, hanging in folds like a turkey's wattles. He absently scratched his ribs. The scratching intensified the itching. Maybe it was the dirt on his shirt making him itch. He was going to have to change it one of these days soon.

16

THE LONG COLD WIND

His eyes were greedy as he stared at old man Larkin's place. He was getting old, and he wanted to settle down. He had been hankering to own a place like this for several years. The notion first took him, when Enoch Parnell claimed most of the land around Larkin. Linus would like to live right in the midst of Enoch Parnell and prick him every time he got the chance. Six years ago, he would have been afraid to entertain any such idea. He wasn't afraid now. Enoch couldn't run him off, if he bought this place legal. The law had come to Montana. It would protect little people like Linus against big people like Enoch.

Cully said, "You must be thinking of Parnell." The old man always got that trapped-wolf look whenever he thought of Parnell. It tickled Cully to see the old man bedeviled that way. In size, he was a replica of his father but carved leaner. He was thick through the shoulders and arms, and he stood on stocky, bandy legs. He was dark, where his father was light, the result of his mother's blood. That blood outcropped in other places, in the high cheekbones, the flattened face, and the black, smoky eyes. He was a half-breed. He knew bad treatment from both Indian and white man because of it. He blamed his father, and when he was drunk he thought of killing him. Two years ago, he had tried it, and Linus had almost broken him in two. Cully still remembered the beating. Someday, he would try it again.

He stared at the cabin. He would like to own something like that. It stood on a fine piece of hay bottom. He guessed the bench to be some two miles long and maybe a half mile wide. If he had this place, he would put a few head of cattle on it. Cattle gave a man standing. His breathing quickened. If Linus could only get this place. The old man couldn't live forever. When he died the place would go to Cully. He didn't dare look at his father. He was afraid the thought would show in his eyes.

"Yes, sir," Linus said in pleased anticipation. "I always wanted that place. Old man Larkin would never listen to any offer. But he'll listen this morning." He beamed at Cully. He had set Cully to watching Larkin six months ago. Cully's Indian blood came in handy for a job like that, for Larkin never suspected a thing. Cully was a good son. His Indian blood made him wild at times, particularly when he was drinking. Linus tried to control the drinking all he could. It was hard to do, when a man made the stuff. He had a daughter who was three years older than Cully. Letty had married Chad Parnell, and it tickled Linus to think of how riled that must be making Enoch. He thought of the Bannock squaw, who had borne him two children. She had been dead a number of years now, and he missed her. Not because of any love but because she kept things a lot cleaner and more orderly than he and Cully could.

He grinned at Cully, displaying the snaggy teeth in the front of his lower jaw. "With us here and Letty right 'amongst them, we'll make the Parnells squirm."

He started toward the cabin. A man wouldn't have to work too hard to live comfortably here. Chokecherries and bullberries lined the creek, and in less than a quarter of a mile, they flushed sage and prairie chicken. The buffalo were almost gone, but a man could find deer in the higher reaches of the mountains.

Old man Larkin had been chopping wood for the cooking stove, and he did not see them until he turned around, his arms full of cut wood. The sight of the two, sitting there, startled him, and he dropped the wood. He hadn't heard the horses. He must be getting deafer every day.

"Goddamn it, Linus," he exploded. "Do you have to Injun up on a man that-a-way?" He put a hasty glance on Cully Derks. That damned Indian never talked. He just watched a man with those dead black eyes until a man's skin started crawling. He said lamely, "I didn't hear you coming."

Linus's grin broadened. "We just rode by to see if you're in a mood for selling." He had hit that poker game in Miles City a couple of nights ago for almost three hundred dollars. He had something to offer Larkin.

Larkin said testily, "I told you I ain't never going to sell. I'm going to die right here." He coughed and thought, I damned near did last winter. He caught the cold early, and he couldn't get rid of it. The cough said it was still lingering. It was hard on an old man living alone. Just the survival chores took a lot out of him. Besides, if he were in a mood to sell, Linus Derks had nothing to buy with. He had never known Derks to have two dollars to rub together.

Larkin picked up his wood and started for the house. "There's no use you riding by here and bothering me."

Linus pulled a cloth sack out of his saddlebag. It clinked pleasantly as he moved it. "There's two hundred and fifty dollars here, Larkin." It would be a fair price. He wanted this deal to be that way. He wanted no kickbacks from it.

Larkin stared at the sack in fascination. He hadn't seen that much money in one pile for years. He said stubbornly, "I ain't selling."

The grin stayed on Linus Derks' face. "Help him make up his mind, Cully."

Cully untied the awkward bundle behind his saddle and let it fall to the ground. It flopped open, and Larkin stared in horror at the brand on the hide. The letters E-P were four inches high. He didn't have to move any closer to read them. He saw the dirt clinging to the hairs of the hide, and for a moment his voice was gone. When he spoke, his voice came out squeaky. "Where did you get that?"

He knew where Derks found it. He knew just where he'd buried it.

Linus jingled the bag. "I'm still offering you this. Or do you want old Parnell to see this hide?"

"You wouldn't do that, Linus," Larkin said frantically. "That steer came right into my yard last winter. I was sick and couldn't hunt. A man's got a right to eat."

"You've been sick a long time, Larkin. Cully knows where you buried two more hides. We can take Parnell to them."

Larkin closed his eyes. He could see the look on Enoch Parnell's face. A shiver ran through him. Parnell was a cold, merciless man. He wouldn't listen to any excuses. Larkin wasn't sure what Parnell would do. He only knew he would do something.

He looked about the place, and it was suddenly strange to him. He was old and tired, and life was getting too big for him to cope with. He had a brother, living in Helena. He could move in with him. Two hundred and fifty dollars would carry him for a long time. He thought of the promise he made Enoch—that if he ever sold, it would be only to him. If he tried to keep that promise, Linus would show Enoch those hides. The least Enoch would do would be to deduct the cost of those steers out of the purchase price. It wasn't fair, taking an old man's money like that, but Enoch would do it. Larkin made up his mind. Linus was here, offering the full amount. Wouldn't a man be a damned fool to accept something less?

He said dully, "I guess I'll sell, Linus."

"I thought you would. Get your horse. We'll ride into Miles City and draw up the papers. I want everything nice and proper."

A pride swelled within him as he waited for Larkin. This was the first piece of land he had ever owned. Enoch Parnell would rave like a wild man at him settling here, and he couldn't do a thing about it.

He said, "Cully, as soon as we move in, we've got some work to do." Parnell drove over this land to reach his summer range. For a half mile, the stream flowed over a gravelly bed with low banks. Stock could cross it anywhere along that half mile. Above and below, the stream deepened, and the banks were sheer, the bottom of the creek muddy. Let Parnell find himself another crossing, let him lose some head in the muddy bottom.

Cully didn't like the sound of the word. "What work?"

"We got to string us some fence." Linus was glad he had money left over from his poker profits. Lack of money sure hamstrung a man.

He grinned at Cully's scowl. "We don't want people crossing our land every time they get a notion to."

Owen said, "I haven't seen old Larkin for almost a month. I hope he's all right."

He didn't miss the flicker of annoyance that crossed his father's face. Larkin was a thorn in Enoch Parnell's side. Enoch had tried often enough to buy Larkin out, and the old man wouldn't sell. Larkin had clung stubbornly to the land he had hacked out of the wilderness, and that was the man's right. A year ago, Enoch had quit offering. Larkin couldn't live forever, and Enoch could wait. One way or another he gets his way, Owen thought.

He saw his father rein in suddenly, and there was shocked surprise on his face. It jerked him out of his thoughts, and he followed his father's eyes. The strands of new barb gleamed bright in the sunlight.

"Why, Goddamn it," Enoch raved. "What the hell does he think he's doing?"

Owen frowned at the fence. Relations between Larkin and the Parnells had always been good, and he wondered why Larkin suddenly felt the need of this fence. The fence cut off the only suitable ford for quite a distance in both directions. Finding another ford could add as much as two days to the drive to summer range. He heard the ring of a hammer coming from beyond a small rise and said, "He's working over there."

Enoch's face had a grim belligerence. "I want to talk to him."

He stopped short as he topped the rise. Owen pulled up beside him. Linus and Cully Derks were stapling wire to a line of freshly set posts. They were working hard. Cully was stripped to the waist and sweat glistened on the big arm and shoulder muscles.

Owen said, "I didn't think there was enough money to make those two work that hard."

Enoch said savagely, "Larkin not only puts up a fence. He hires miserable help to do it. By God, I'm going to get to the bottom of this."

Owen watched the Derkses move to another post. Not so miserable help, he thought. He would hate to be held to that pace all day.

Enoch started his horse, and Cully heard the small sound of the hoofs. He touched his father on the shoulder, and both men turned. Cully's face was impassive. Owen had the feeling a wary waiting was behind it. Linus beamed at them all the way from the top of the hill to the fence.

"Howdy, Enoch," he said. "Light and sit." The smile was all over his face—except in his eyes. His eyes hated with a cold malevolence.

"Where's Larkin?" Enoch demanded.

Linus took a deliberate time in laying down his hammer. He rolled a cigarette, and there was insolence in the amount of time he used. This was his big moment, and he was enjoying himself.

Owen saw the rage tightening the cords in his father's neck. Linus Derks wasn't very smart, baiting Enoch like this.

Enoch snapped, "Answer me." The words sounded like two pieces of gravel being rubbed together.

Linus lifted his face to him. "Why, didn't you know, Enoch? Larkin's gone. We're neighbors now." He liked the sound of the word, and he repeated it. "Neighbors."

The word hit Enoch like a club. It stunned his thinking, and he had trouble finding his tongue. "Neighbors," he repeated blankly. "You're not living here."

Linus bobbed his head. "We are. Moved in two weeks ago. How do you like the improvement we've been making?" He waved at the fence, and a slyness crept into his smile.

Enoch threw off and rushed him. He seized Linus by the shirt front, and his face was twisted with fury. "What have you done with Larkin? If you've harmed him, I'll kill you."

Cully growled deep in his throat and made a move.

"Hold it," Owen snapped. Something was drastically wrong. Linus still looked as though he enjoyed this, and he should be frightened.

Linus struck Enoch's hands away, and his face looked injured. "I don't call that being neighborly at all, Enoch. I bought this place from Larkin."

The effrontery of it tied up Enoch's tongue. No one could buy this place from Larkin. "You're a liar," he sputtered.

Linus fumbled in his shirt pocket. "I oughta sue you for that, Enoch. I got the papers here in my pocket. Everything's proper." He pulled out a well-creased paper. It looked as though he had been carrying it around for some time for just such a moment as this.

Enoch's face went slack as he unfolded and read it.

Linus said, "You know Larkin's signature. There it is."

Enoch shook his head helplessly. "He wouldn't sell. He wouldn't sell to anybody. You forced him to sign and then killed him."

Linus glared at him. "Sheriff John Kilmonte signed that paper as a witness. I'm getting tired of your lies about me. You've called me a squaw man. You got me run out of Deer Lodge, calling me a horse thief." Naked hating replaced the false beaming.

Enoch breathed like a man after a hard run. "They should have hanged you, instead of letting you go." His eyes went to Cully and swung contemptuously back to Linus. "You are a squaw man."

The hating between the two flowed like strong currents. Cully was in on it, too. It seemed to spill out of his pores. It would be easy for Cully to hate, Owen thought. But Cully's hate wouldn't be selective. It would include every white man.

The false beam was back on Linus's face. "A man wants to be as close to his daughter as he can, Enoch. You know, we're kinda related by marriage."

He poured handfuls of salt into a raw wound. Enoch looked like he was choking. "Don't press on that relationship, Linus. Because your daughter's at my house doesn't mean you'll ever be welcome there."

Linus's face turned violent. "By God, you stay off my land, too."

"Enoch," Owen called sharply. He was afraid an open clash couldn't be averted.

Enoch glared at him, then turned and stalked to his horse. He mounted and faced Derks. His face was impassive. He had control of himself. "There's something going on here I don't know about. But I'll find out about it. I'll talk to Kilmonte."

Linus cackled in sheer pleasure. Even Cully's lip corners twitched.

They've got something on their side, Owen thought. They're too damned sure of themselves.

"You do that," Linus said. "You ride in and talk to the sheriff." His cackling laughter followed the two riders.

"It's all legal," Kilmonte said. "Larkin sold out to Linus. Linus insisted upon me as a witness." He was a short man with shoulders so massive they made him look misshapen. In some past time, his nose had been broken. It had set with a pronounced hump and was out of line, giving his face a lopsided look. He had cold, gray eyes and a hard mouth. Kilmonte wouldn't take pushing around from anybody. His eyes were filled with dislike as he looked at Enoch.

It's an old dislike, Owen thought. They crossed paths somewhere back.

"Something's wrong," Enoch said stubbornly. "Larkin wouldn't sell to me. He wouldn't sell to that scum."

Kilmonte's tone was weary. "He did sell. For two hundred and fifty dollars. It was a fair price."

"Derks had him scared then," Enoch insisted. "After the deal was completed, Derks killed him."

Kilmonte threw up his hands. "Oh, good God. I put Larkin on the stage to Helena. I saw it pull out. And don't tell me Linus met the stage somewhere down the road. He didn't leave town until the next day."

Owen watched the baffled look in Enoch's eyes. Enoch was up against something he could not understand or handle.

"I won't have it," Enoch said. "I won't have that lawless scum living next to me. I'll watch every step he makes. The first wrong one, and I'll—"

"You'll do nothing," Kilmonte said. He leveled a finger at Enoch, and his eyes looked like icicle points. "You got any complaints against the Derkses, you bring them to me."

The two locked eyes, and Enoch's face was wild. "By God, I know where you stand now, Kilmonte."

He turned and stomped out of the office, and Owen started to follow him.

Kilmonte said, "Just a minute, Owen."

Owen swung around to face him, and Kilmonte studied his face. He sighed and said, "At least, you're not boiling like he is. Owen, if you have any influence on him, steady him down. He's done as he's damned pleased all his life. He can't do it any more."

Owen was torn between loyalty and fairness. The fairness won. He shrugged and said, "John, do you know anybody who tells Enoch what to do?"

Kilmonte said, "I guess not. But he's going to obey the law. The same as anybody else." He saw the protest in Owen's eyes and grinned wearily. "He's no murderer or thief. But he's not going to run over anybody else. I know what the Derkses are. And I'll handle them. Not Enoch. This deal puzzles me as much as it does him. But it's legal, and like it or not, he's going to have to live next to them."

Owen nodded. He could live next to the Derkses and not choke every time he saw them. Enoch might have more trouble in making the adjustment. "I'll get Molly to talk to him."

Kilmonte nodded. "You do that. Maybe she can keep that old bull from busting out of his corral." He walked to the door with Owen. Owen had the sudden feeling this man had a lonely job. Kilmonte could not afford to be too friendly with anyone.

Kilmonte touched his misshapen nose. "You can't like him but you've got to respect him. Do you know he gave me this?"

He grinned bleakly at the surprise on Owen's face and nodded. "Twenty-five years ago in Hell Gate. He was doing a lot of trading with the emigrant trains, trying to get a start in cattle. Frenchy LeBaron's horses broke through a fence and got at his haystacks. Enoch shot one of them. We were trying to establish law and order, and I think that was the first case ever tried in Montana. I was sent to bring him in. We had quite a scuffle. He came with me."

Owen's lips moved in a faint smile. In his way, John Kilmonte was as determined a man as Enoch Parnell.

"We tried to do everything proper," Kilmonte said. "We held the trial in Holt's saloon. We had a judge and a jury, and I think every man on that jury was worried about what Enoch was thinking about them. The prosecutor made some remarks about good citizenship that Enoch took personal. He stood up and cussed out the judge, he cussed out the jury." Kilmonte shook his head. "It started the damnedest brawl I ever saw. Before it was over everybody was in on it. That fight broke up the trial."

"Owen," Enoch bawled from outside.

"I'm coming," Owen yelled. He looked at Kilmonte. "The trial was dropped."

"No, we held it next day. Enoch was found guilty and fined forty dollars. He wasn't there. Everybody sorta forgot to go out and get him. The fine was never collected, either."

Owen laughed. If Kilmonte hadn't put a name to the principal in the case, he could have named him. Enoch Parnell.

Kilmonte grinned wryly. "He got away with it twenty-five years ago. He might have gotten away with it ten years ago. But that time has passed, and he's got to realize it. Two weeks after his trial he dragged in Linus Derks by the collar and accused him of stealing one of his horses. He wanted to see how damned good our court was. He didn't have any proof. We had to turn Linus free."

"Was he guilty?"

Kilmonte shrugged. "He probably was. He's done about everything in the book. He's been a horse and cow thief. He's been a whiskey peddler. I don't know how many Indians he's started on the warpath by filling them full of his rotgut."

"Owen," Enoch roared. "I'm not waiting the whole morning."

"Coming," Owen called back.

"I'm not blaming Enoch for his hating the Derkses," Kilmonte said. "He's got enough reason. But he can't handle things himself any more. You tell him that."

"I'll tell him, John." It wouldn't do any good. Nobody told Enoch Parnell anything.

His father was mounted, when Owen walked outside. He saw the cold, angry look in Enoch's eyes and thought, he'll burn over this for days.

He swung into the saddle, and Enoch asked, "What were you talking about?"

"Nothing."

Enoch's eyes darkened. "It took all that time to talk about nothing."

Owen shrugged.

Enoch spat in the direction of Kilmonte's office. "The Goddamned, worthless law," he said.

THREE

The sound of quarreling voices awakened Owen in the morning. His bedroom was next to Chad and Letty's, and the wall wasn't thick enough. They quarreled a lot for a six-month-old married couple. He lay there and listened. Most of the quarreling came from Letty's side. A pleading note kept creeping into Chad's voice. That was a strange thing to hear from Chad. He had always been hot-headed, ready to fight at even the suggestion of an affront.

Owen still couldn't get used to the idea of Chad being married to her. Oh, she was attractive enough. She could pull a man's eyes. Owen had danced with her several times in town, but he never had a serious thought about her.

He swung his feet to the floor and began dressing. He hated to hear Chad begging. If that was what marriage did to a man, he didn't want any part of it. If the quarreling kept on, he was going to move to the bunkhouse.

He tugged on his boots. Only silence came from the next door room. He supposed Chad had pacified her. He had heard a lot of those silences, too. They were usually preceded by giggles and Chad's happy laughter. That was harder to take than the quarreling. It made Owen restless and lonely.

He walked into the kitchen, and Molly was frying ham. A bowl of batter stood next to a smoking frying pan. His stomach rumbled pleasantly. Molly was cooking ham and pancakes, Enoch's favorite breakfast. For two days, she had served only his favorite foods.

Owen put his arms around his mother and hugged her. A rush of affection seized him, and he picked her up and whirled her around.

"You put me down," she scolded. "This minute. You hear me? Do you want me to ruin breakfast?"

Her eyes were shining as she looked up at her son. If Owen never received affection from his father, he received it from his mother. She was a small woman, now growing a little plump. She was twenty-two years younger than Enoch, and Owen often wondered how she had ever fallen in love with him. The course of love took some strange paths. Streaks of gray were beginning to appear in her dark hair, and it hurt Owen every time he looked at them. She was a sweet-faced woman with a mouth built for laughter. She had to make her own, for Enoch never gave her any help along that line. She was the stabilizing factor in this household; she kept them from cutting each other's throats.

He heard Enoch's voice, outside, bellowing orders for the day's work. He didn't have to ask if Enoch were still angry. Enoch always roared his orders when he was mad.

Molly was watching him, and Owen shrugged and grinned. "It'll wear off someday, I guess."

She frowned at him before she began ladling batter into the frying pan. She always defended Enoch, whenever she could. Owen watched her busy hands. She had a gift of timing. When Enoch stepped into the kitchen, Molly would have a stack of smoking pancakes ready for him.

Enoch walked into the kitchen and hung his hat on a peg. He didn't speak or nod to either of them. Owen slid into his seat across the table from his father. He kept his eyes fastened on the table. He was quivering with anger, and if he looked at Enoch, it would show. It wouldn't change anything, it would only make matters harder for Molly.

Enoch forked the stack of cakes onto his plate. "Is that damned boy still in bed?"

Owen thought, Linus beat him, and he'll take it out on Chad and Letty.

Molly said, "He'll be right in, Enoch."

"Ever since he got married, he spends all his time in bed," Enoch said.

Owen tensed. Enoch dug up the old subject every chance he found.

"Enoch," Molly protested.

"If he wanted her that bad, five dollars would have bought her."

Molly slammed her palm against the table. Hot spots of anger glowed in her cheeks. "That's enough of that, Enoch Parnell. They're married. And nothing you can do will change it."

Owen expected a savage outbreak, and it didn't come. It always amazed him to see Molly shut up the old man. That had been a bad night, six months ago. Chad hadn't been home for three days, and Molly was beginning to worry. Owen wanted to go look for Chad, and Enoch refused to let him go. "He's old enough to know the way home," Enoch said. "If he don't know it, let him stay lost."

Owen remembered the moment Chad came through the door. Letty Derks was with him. Chad had tried to be light about it, but his lips had trembled. "Pa. Ma," he said. "Meet the new Mrs. Parnell. We got married in Miles City three days ago."

The announcement froze them. Enoch's face was thunderstruck, and Molly's was sick. Owen remembered how Chad's arm slid protectively about Letty's shoulders.

Enoch had raved and cursed, and Molly had to yell at him a half-dozen times before she could make him shut up. She tried to smile at Letty, and her shaking lips couldn't hold the expression. "Chad," she said. "Take Letty to your room."

Letty's eyes were on the floor as she crossed the room. Chad followed close behind her as though he were glad to escape.

"I won't have her here," Enoch bellowed. "I won't have any daughter of Derks in my house."

Molly looked as though she had suddenly grown six inches as she faced him. "They're married. It's done. You'll accept her for Chad's sake."

"I'll throw him out, too," Enoch roared.

"Then I go with them."

Enoch's jaw slackened. He looked as dazed as though he had been hit with a club.

"I mean it," Molly said quietly.

Enoch never spoke for the rest of the evening. It was a bad

evening. It was followed by a lot of bad evenings. Enoch never again spoke directly to Letty. Whenever he wanted to tell her something, he relayed his words through Molly. Owen had seen Letty look at Enoch with naked hating in her eyes. The house was filled with constant hating. It was pulling it to pieces.

Molly didn't like Letty, either, though she never lost her patience with her. Letty couldn't keep her and Chad's bedroom clean, and every meal she cooked was a mess. She liked to spend hours before a mirror, and she shirked every task Molly set her. Molly gave up trying after a couple of months. It was easier doing the work herself, than keeping after Letty.

Owen heard Chad and Letty come into the kitchen. He didn't look around until Chad said, "—morning, everybody."

Chad's hair was tousled, his shirt only half buttoned. His eyes were shining. He looked like a happy man, a satisfied man. Letty had a power over him, too much power. She could lift him from misery to happiness in a few seconds and plunge him back as quickly. Her hair looked messed, too, and her eyes were on the floor. Owen saw the smile playing about her lips. She rarely spoke, when Enoch was around.

Enoch said bitingly, "I thought you were going to stay in bed all day."

Chad's face turned sullen, and Owen gripped the table edge. Enoch never let up on Chad any more. For six months, he had pushed him savagely, both mentally and physically. He had always been hard on Chad, but he excelled himself the past months.

Chad took the chair next to his father, and Letty sat down on Chad's left. Chad was eighteen, and with the sulky look on his face he looked his age. He was shaving but not too often. Last week's cut was still scabbed over. He wasn't as tall as Enoch or Owen, and immaturity still held his face. He had a wild temper, and knowing Chad as he did, Owen thought it amazing Chad kept a check on it as well as he did. But someday Enoch would push him too far.

Letty was something to look at. Owen thought she was older than Chad, maybe by as much as five or six years. Her hair was the blackest Owen had ever seen, and it had a shine to it. Her Indian blood showed up in her dusky skin and brilliant black eyes. Letty was at the peak of physical ripeness. It wasn't hard to understand how Chad had lost his head over her. It made Owen uncomfortable to be around her. Not that he actually coveted her, but she displayed too much of herself. She wore as few clothes as she could, and many a day Owen suspected she had nothing on beneath her dress. She usually went barelegged, and she wore her skirts shorter than other women. She would suddenly spin, apparently for no reason but a quick delight, and the skirt would fly out, exposing firm thighs. Her blouses were generally too loose, and when she bent over, most of her breasts showed. Molly was aware of it, too. Owen had heard her trying to talk to Letty about it. She hadn't done much good. This morning was an example. Letty's blouse kept slipping off one shoulder. It was a beautifully turned shoulder. Owen stayed away from her as much as he could. He didn't want to add to Chad's misery.

Molly put pancakes on all the plates and sat down. Owen kept his attention on his eating. Chad, he thought mournfully. You messed up my life, too, by bringing her here. He had intended asking Evlalie Denton to marry him this spring. Three years was long enough to go with a girl. But he couldn't bring her here into all this discord. He had to wait until things leveled out a little. He felt a sudden flare of anger against Chad. Damn you, Chad. You could have waited. You've got more time than I have. His silence was affecting his relations with Evlalie. The last few months she had been distinctly cold and distant.

Molly got up and put another stack of cakes on Enoch's plate.

Enoch said pointedly, "It seems like somebody else could do a little work around here once in a while."

Letty jumped to her feet, and Molly said soothingly, "It's all right. Everything's done."

Letty sat down. She gave Enoch one brief, furious glance.

Enoch poured syrup over his cakes. "Owen, get the meat house ready. We're going to butcher this afternoon."

Fresh beef would be a welcome change. Owen nodded without speaking.

Enoch flicked his eyes at Chad. "Chad, check the fence around the hay meadow. I saw some sagging wire yesterday."

It was a long, monotonous job. It could mean a lot of walking, if many staples were out. Usually, the job fell to one of the hands.

Dismay flooded Chad's face. "But I promised Letty "

Enoch's eyes bored into him. "You promised what?"

Owen saw the sullen droop of Letty's mouth. The two had

planned something for the day. Letty would punish Chad tonight for the disappointment. The misery would be on his face in the morning.

"Nothing," Chad said. He rose, shoved back his plate, and stalked for the door.

"Come back here and finish your breakfast," Enoch ordered.

"I'm not hungry." That was anger in Chad's voice.

Enoch's face hardened at the tone. His sons didn't talk to him that way.

The meal was finished in uncomfortable silence. Owen was glad when it was over. He said, "I'd better be getting at that meat house."

He walked outside and Scotty was just cinching his saddle. Scotty had been with them for six years. He was a middle-aged, balding man with a powerful chest and short, bowed legs. His loyalty to the E-P was enduring. That loyalty was a peculiar thing. It suffered hardships and privation, yet Scotty would have been surprised if someone had asked him why. Owen thought, maybe it's because a cowpuncher doesn't know any better.

Scotty grinned and asked, "What's wrong with Chad? He tore past me like his tail was on fire."

Owen shrugged. Scotty couldn't help but know what was going on, but Owen didn't feel like discussing it with him. Scotty was a friend, almost a member of the family, but not quite.

Scotty said, "I'd better be going. The old man wants a report on the summer range. We're going to be in trouble, if we don't get some rain pretty soon."

Owen said soberly, "We are."

Enoch came out of the house and frowned at them. Scotty swung hastily into the saddle. The old man had been touchy the last few days. A wise man didn't give him an excuse to find fault. Scotty raised a hand to Owen and galloped off.

Owen walked toward the meat house. He had a tedious job ahead of him. He had to check every crack, every possible entrance to make it flyproof. No matter how thorough he was, a few flies always got in. He hated a damned blowfly. They ruined so much meat. He put them in the same class as a magpie. The raucous black-and-white bird would peck at a scratch on a cow and enlarge it to a running sore. Then the blowflies moved in, and if they weren't caught in time, you had a dead animal on your hands. Magpies and blowflies worked together. Add wolves to the list, Owen thought. A wolf's killing was cleaner and more direct, but it still amounted to a loss. There was always something to plague a man.

He tore down the old mosquito netting over the windows and replaced it with new. He checked the fit of the door and windows. He looked for cracks in the boards. He was absorbed in his work, when he heard the door open. He turned, and Letty was coming through the door.

"What are you doing here?" His tone was sharper than he intended.

He saw the withdrawing in her face and felt an instant's contriteness. Her life here couldn't be too happy.

She said sullenly, "I just wanted to see what you were doing." She gave him a covert glance. She wished she were married to him instead of Chad. Chad was such a kid. Could it be one of the reasons she had married Chad—to be near Owen? She mentally shrugged. She was near him, and it hadn't done her much good.

Owen said, "I was trying to make this flyproof." He heard a buzzing and saw a fly settle on the mosquito netting.

"Damn it," he said. "How did he get in here?" He hit it with his hat, and it fell to the floor. He stepped on it with his boot. It probably came in when Letty opened the door.

She moved a step closer to him, and her blouse had slipped again, exposing that bare, rounded shoulder. She didn't wear perfume, but a scent came from her, the raw, primitive scent of woman.

She said, "One fly?" and shrugged. He was making a lot of fuss over a single fly.

"They blow meat, Letty. They bore into it and lay their eggs. That part of the meat's ruined." He kept on talking about flies. It was a safe subject.

"Flies are about the toughest form of life I know of, Letty. When cold weather sets in, they crawl behind loose bark on dead trees, or into any crack that will give them shelter. They freeze solid, and you think they're dead. But when the chinook comes and it begins to thaw, they come out as alive as ever. They can go through a dozen freezes that way."

He heard another buzz, and a fly lit on the mosquito netting. The sun shone on its green, metallic back. Letty didn't let that one in. They were getting in somehow, and he would have sworn the building was flyproof.

He killed the fly and looked at the netting on the south window. A half-dozen flies crawled on the outside of it. They didn't get in that way, they couldn't get through the netting.

As he watched, one of the flies poked its front legs through a mesh of the netting. It pulled the mesh apart enough to get its head through, then, wiggling and squirming, forced its body through the tiny opening. The mesh sprang back into place behind it.

"The sonsofbitches," Owen exploded. He didn't think of apologizing to Letty. His attention was on the fly problem. Mosquito netting wasn't going to keep them out.

The door opened, and Enoch stepped into the building. He looked at Owen, then at Letty, and his eyes were coldly suspicious.

"What's going on here?" he demanded.

Owen said, "We were watching to see how the flies get in here. They force their way through the netting."

"Is that all she's got to do?" Enoch asked. "I saw an empty pail outside the door."

Letty's lips made that sullen, downward curve. "I came out for a bucket of water. I thought I could help Owen."

"Tell her to get the water," Enoch said. He glared at her until she left the building.

"Why don't you go a little easy on her?" Owen asked.

That baleful look was in Enoch's eyes. "I don't want her in my house." He couldn't order her out because Chad would leave. And if Chad left, Molly would follow him. Her threat had never been repeated, but Enoch knew it still stood. The frustration was boiling, back of his eyes.

He said, "And I don't want you hanging around her. It's bad enough she's got Chad."

It took a moment for the implication to hit Owen, then the angry blood congested in his face. "Are you saying—"

"I'm not saying anything," Enoch snapped. "But I know breed women. We got enough trouble on our hands." He turned and stalked out of the building.

Owen picked up his hammer and threw it through the mosquito netting. The damned stuff was no good, anyhow.

FOUR

The spring roundup was behind them. Owen was appointed captain and received two dollars and fifty cents a day. At his age, it was quite an honor. He gave orders impartially to every man, including Enoch and Chad. It surprised him that Enoch took those orders without a flicker of resentment. He worked from dawn to dark, correlating the details. He checked on the circle riders moving out in every direction early in the morning. He watched them bring the cattle back to the corral, where the ropers threw the ones to be branded. The wrestlers and the men with the smoking irons branded and marked the bawling animal, then thrust the iron back into the fire to reheat. It was hard, fast work. A man's day was filled with dust and heat and the smell of singed hair. It was a permeating smell, and he never got it out of his nostrils. Food even seemed to taste of it. All day long, a man's ears were blasted by the bellowing of hundreds of cattle until his head rang under the pounding. At night, he was glad to eat his meal wearily and crawl into his blankets.

The roundup lasted four weeks and showed a disappointing tally. Everybody suffered heavy winter losses, and the weakened cows did not bear well. A weakened cow was also easy prey for wolves. The gray devils traveled in bands of twenty to thirty, and cattle were afraid of them. They ran at the sight of one, and the wolves' superior speed and endurance made it an easy matter to overtake and drag them down. A cow would fight to protect her calf, but she was a poor match for even one large wolf.

In the few short minutes before sleep, men talked about the heat and the short grass and the possibility of another severe winter. Some of them worried, and others refused to look squarely at present conditions. Even if they admitted they were bad, they said it would change.

Clell Sawtelle came to Owen on the last day of the roundup. Sawtelle was manager of the Mountain Cattle Company, a paper manager, for he had little knowledge of the practical or working side of the cattle business. He cheerfully admitted it and could laugh at his own mistakes. He represented English money, and his accent stood out oddly against the rougher jargon of the cattle country. He was thirty and looked younger. He was apple-cheeked and blue-eyed. He had brilliant white teeth, and he displayed them often in a flashing smile. He wore English riding boots and fancy foxed riding breeches. Cattlemen laughed at his manners and dress, but they learned to accept him. He was eager to learn the business, and he listened avidly to instruction. Women were drawn by his manners and consideration. Owen had heard his mother say, "I never saw such manners. At first, I didn't think they were real." Sawtelle had been the butt of many rough jokes, but he could laugh at them and at himself. Owen could say bleakly that the man was popular.

Sawtelle said, "I say, old chap, but you've handled things well."

Owen bristled. Then he saw Sawtelle wasn't condescending but meant it as sincere praise. He did not like the man. He knew he was being unfair, and he knew the basis of it. He had found Sawtelle at Evlalie Denton's house too many times. And too often, he had heard Evlalie and Sawtelle laughing together. Ev seemed too absorbed in the man. Sawtelle was an interesting talker, and he had seen much of the world. Owen always felt tongue-tied when the man was around.

He grunted in reply to Sawtelle's praise.

Sawtelle ignored the rudeness. He grimaced and said, "It wasn't a good roundup, was it? My associates will be unhappy when they get my report."

Sawtelle's associates did none of the work and suffered none of the hardships, but they expected big profits. Owen resented all foreign money for that reason.

He said sharply, "They'll be getting worse reports, if everybody keeps crowding the range with more cattle."

"Ah," Sawtelle said. "So you are one of the pessimistic chaps. Your father doesn't believe that way."

"He can believe the way he wants to," Owen said curtly.

I am inclined to agree with your father. All we need is rain. I believe in this country so much that we're putting five thousand more head on the range this fall."

Sawtelle sat in his big house and wrote glowing reports to his associates abroad. All he could see was the endless profits. It wasn't fair to blame Sawtelle alone, for other men were doing the same thing, men who should know better. Even my father, Owen thought. There had to be a saturation point, and Owen thought they were rapidly reaching it. When it came, a lot of people were going to go broke.

Owen said, "I never saw so many men so damned eager to cut their own throats." He walked away, leaving Sawtelle staring after him in surprise.

He hoped they could wind this up in an hour or two. He wanted to get back to the home ranch by nightfall. He wanted to ride over and see Evlalie.

He was luckier than he thought. He was home by six o'clock. He ate a hasty supper, bathed, and put on his best clothes. He shined the new pair of boots twice before he was satisfied with them. He snitched some of Molly's cologne and grinned at himself in the mirror. A man knew how much he missed a girl, when he was away from her for four weeks.

He walked outside, and the four E-P punchers were mounted, ready for the ride into town. Each was dressed in his best, and their eyes shone with delight at the prospect of the evening ahead of them. They would come home broke and with oversized heads and consider the evening worth it.

Les Moyer said, "You coming with us, Owen?"

Scotty said, "Hell no, he's not coming with us. Look at the way he's dressed. Can't you guess where he's going?"

Abel Brockton put a mock study on his face. "Give me three guesses. Maybe I can hit it."

Owen growled, "Get along." His grin wouldn't let the growl ring true.

Hamp Stoner reined his horse several steps nearer Owen and

leaned out of his saddle toward him. He sniffed several times and said, "Phewy. What's that I smell?"

Scotty moved closer, sniffed, and said, "Hydrophoby skunk, maybe. No gal is going to get close to a man who smells like that."

"That's enough," Owen yelled. "I'll call Enoch out here. He'll sure as hell find something for you to do."

They looked at each other in mock consternation. "He's just dirty enough to call the old man," Les said. "We'd better get while we can."

They spun and spurred their horses, and Owen stepped out of the dust they raised. Their whooping drifted back to him for several seconds.

He was still smiling as he mounted and turned his horse toward Evlalie's. They were good men, all four of them. They earned whatever little pleasure they could find.

He hummed a tune all the way to the Denton place. The tune stopped abruptly as he saw the horse tied at the rack in front of the house. It was Sawtelle's claybank gelding, and Owen muttered a soft curse.

Evlalie answered his knock. A quick flash of some emotion appeared in her eyes. Owen could not say what it was. Anger maybe, he thought gloomily. At my interruption.

He followed her into the parlor, and Sawtelle beamed at him. He said, "You look fresh, old man," as though he were surprised Owen could even move.

Owen felt heat in his face. Did Sawtelle think he was the only man capable of riding somewhere after several weeks of hard work?

Evlalie asked, "How did it go, Owen?" She was a tall, slender girl but ample where a woman should be ample. Her chestnut hair had a gloss to it, and when the sun struck it, it dug up red highlights. Her eyes were brown, splashed with tiny flecks of gold. Her mouth was too generous for classic beauty, but it was a laughing mouth. She was a competent woman. She could turn out a meal that would delight any man, and she could chop and split the wood to cook it with. She was two years younger than Owen, but at times, he thought he would never catch up to her wisdom. Women seemed to be born with an instinctive wisdom that men struggled all their lives to acquire.

He said, "All right." He didn't mean it to be abrupt. He wanted to tell her about it, he was eager to speak of his responsibility, but Sawtelle's presence tongue-tied him.

Sawtelle said, "He was appointed captain. He did a jolly good job in keeping everything moving."

Evlalie put a quick glance on Owen, then looked back to Sawtelle.

Sawtelle talked for a half hour about the roundup. He saw humor in little mishaps that Owen overlooked, and he had Evlalie laughing often. Owen sat there, feeling dull and lonely. He answered "yes" or "no" to the occasional question tossed his way. He thought the last time Evlalie looked at him her eyes were filled with annoyance.

He waited ten minutes to find the lull he wanted. He asked, "Ev, is Tom around?"

She gave him a long, level look, and he wished he knew the thoughts behind those probing eyes.

She said quietly, "He's in the kitchen."

Owen stood. He felt as if he were all hands and feet. "I've got to talk to him about something."

Sawtelle said, "It's been nice talking to you. I'll see you again, old man."

Owen turned and plunged for the kitchen.

Tom Denton read a newspaper by the light of the kerosene lamp. His glasses were on the tip of his nose, and it looked as though he peered over them instead of through them. Addie Denton was on the other side of the table, rocking comfortably back and forth as she knitted.

Denton looked up and said, "Owen. I didn't hear you come in. Guess I didn't expect you tonight." He shook his head. "It was all I could do to crawl off my horse and stagger into the house. These bones are getting old." Sparse flesh hung unevenly on a big, angular frame. Denton needed a shave, and his beard looked grizzled in the lamplight. His face looked tired. No, it wasn't so much the face as the eyes. His eyes were tired because of some burden of spirit.

The smell of baking gingerbread filled the big kitchen.

"It'll come out of the oven pretty soon, Owen," Addie said. "I thought Clell and Evlalie would like some later on." She never missed a stitch or a rock as she talked. Traces of beauty still remained in her face, though age was beginning to overshadow it. Streaks of gray were beginning to appear in her brown hair.

Evlalie would look like this, when she reached Addie's age. It wasn't a disturbing thought at all. Addie Denton was still an attractive woman.

Owen said, "I'm not hungry." He thought rebelliously: he sure wasn't hungry for gingerbread baked for Clell Sawtelle.

Add cocked her head as a burst of laughter drifted from the parlor. She was unconscious of the smile on her face as she said, "That Clell Sawtelle is a real entertaining man."

She approves of him, Owen thought bleakly. A mother's approval was always important to a daughter.

Tom Denton said dubiously, "I don't know. He's always so damned cheerful. I say it isn't normal, a man always being cheerful."

Addie sniffed at the criticism. "I just wish a little of it would rub off on some people I know."

Denton's face set in an argumentative expression. "You just tell me what I got to be cheerful about. I told you that roundup was bad. I told you how many calves we lost. We get a bad summer and a bad winter, and it'll be worse."

Owen said, "It's going to be worse, if we don't quit overstocking the range. Sawtelle's company is bringing in five thousand more head. Enoch has contracted for two thousand more."

"No," Denton shouted. "Are they crazy?"

Addie said, "Keep your voice down. Are you telling Owen or the people in Miles City?"

Denton gave her an annoyed glance, but he lowered his voice. His face was gloomy. "I just hope to God this weather straightens out. If it doesn't and the damned fools don't stop pretty soon, all of us can be busted right out of business."

Owen had never talked to Denton before about this. He was glad to find someone who believed as he did. "They can't be stopped, Tom. It's free range."

"It won't be so Goddamned free, if it costs us everything we own."

"Tom," Addie said sharply. "You're home now."

He didn't even look at her. "It's got me worried, Owen."

Owen nodded. That made two of them. They talked for twenty minutes of the poor range conditions with two mouths to eat the grass where one mouth had eaten it before. The range could only produce so much grass. But men could keep shoving limitless numbers of cattle onto it.

Addie got up and took the gingerbread out of the oven. She said pointedly, "Give me a cheerful man any time."

Owen stood and said, "I've got to be getting home. Hard day tomorrow."

Denton said, "Not me. I'm going to lay around all day." He cut his eyes at Addie and grinned. "If she doesn't find something for me to do."

Addie watched Owen with speculative eyes. They were probing eyes, and he felt as though she could read his thoughts. They made him feel uncomfortable.

He said, "I'll just slip out the back door. Will you tell Evlalie good night for me?"

He sighed as he closed the door behind him. Addie probably knew everything that was going on. And Owen didn't feel she was sympathetic to his part in it.

He hummed no tune on the way home.

FIVE

The drought's iron grip tightened. Its fingers dug into the creeks and water holes, lowering their contents until the remaining water could no longer dilute the strong alkaline taste. In places, the taste was so strong that thirsty horses and cattle refused to drink it. The short grass was dry and parched, looking as yellowed as it did in late fall. The thermometer kept climbing, and men met with shaking heads saying they had never seen anything like it. The sun made its pitiless orbit day after day, and the hot winds shrieked with glee, their burning tongues sucking every drop of moisture out of the land. Plant life drooped, then wilted, then died, and the land cracked and split, the scars running in all directions, leaving it weary-looking and lined, like an old, tired, careworn face.

The range riders began to find dead cattle, dead from eating poisonous plants. When the grass was eaten out, the weeds came. The weeds were drought-resistant and remained green. Cattle could not resist their green deadly temptation and ate. Among the weeds were the poisonous ones, and cattle died with a huge bellyache that left them in agonized positions.

Letty rode toward her father's cabin. Beads of sweat were on her upper lip, and she could feel it trickling down from her armpits. She thought of McDonald creek with a sudden longing. If there was a deep pool left, she would go for a swim. She rarely visited her father. She did not like him well enough to want to see him often. But anything would be better than the Parnell house. The Parnells sat around with long faces and talked of nothing but cattle. Chad reported last night he had found six more head dead, and Owen had cursed until Molly sharply reminded him where he was. Making that much out of six dead head, Letty thought, when they had all those numbers.

No one talked to her any more. She lived in that house, but she was not a part of it. She was more of an outsider than the evening she first stepped through the door. Damn them all, she thought with a sudden violence. Chad's insistent demands used to irritate her, but for the past month there had been no demand at all. When she had tried to interest him, he had pushed her away, saying he was so tired. Enoch treated her as though she did not exist, and Owen never looked at her. She thought of Owen with mixed anger and longing. If she could make him look at her just once as a man should look at a woman— Her breast rose and fell in sudden, gusty breathing. She needed him to look at her like that. It was a challenge, a standard she needed to establish to restore her self-respect.

Cully saw her coming and had the wires down so that her horse could step over them. She waited while he restapled the wires and said crossly, "Wouldn't it be simpler to put a gate there?"

Cully grinned at her. "And make it easier for the Parnells?"

It was an obsession with both Cully and Linus, a foolish obsession. She asked scornfully, "What makes you think they're interested in your little piece of land?"

"The passage to the mountains," he said. "They'll come someday."

He walked beside her horse toward the cabin. Something was wrong for her to use that tone to him, and her face looked unhappy. It hurt him to see that look. There had always been a close bond between them, closer than ordinary brother and sister, and he thought, our blood shares the same problems. He had been proud and happy when she married Chad Parnell. Her struggles were over. Now looking at her face he was not so sure.

He helped her dismount and turned her horse loose. The grass was still green along the banks of the creek. The horse would not go far.

She stepped inside the cabin and looked about her with disgust. Linus was asleep in one of the bunks, his mouth open with his snoring. She contrasted the appearance of this place with the house Molly Parnell kept, and for a fleeting moment, she appreciated Molly.

She shook Linus awake, and he sat up and yawned, his face truculent at being disturbed.

"Don't you ever clean up this place?" she asked.

Anger showed in Linus's eyes. Letty was putting on airs since she became a Parnell.

He said, "You didn't keep a place any better, when you were with us."

She did not answer, but wandered about the room, her anger plainly apparent. Linus knew alarm. It looked as though something had gone wrong over at the Parnells, and he didn't want it to go wrong. As long as she lived there it gave him a certain immunity. Enoch Parnell might hate him being here, but he would do nothing about it unless Linus committed some flagrant act, an act so bold Enoch could no longer overlook it. Linus intended upon committing no such act. He made and sold a little whiskey to the Indians, but he was clever where he sold it. He took it across the line and sold it to the British treaty Indians, and he never sold it in such quantities that an entire tribe became roaring drunk. He took a certain amount and no matter how much they pleaded for more he didn't have it. The authorities were never aroused, they didn't come looking for the man who sold the whiskey. He had a batch mixing in the shed now. It didn't taste quite right, and he frowned in concentration, trying to think of what he might have left out. The Indians liked their whiskey raw and fiery. They didn't consider it potent unless it burned all the way down. He had started with the usual four gallons of pure spirits. He had put in the five pounds of plug tobacco and poured in two cans of cayenne pepper. He made some mountain sage tea, then added enough water to fill the barrel. Maybe it needed the kick of some more pepper. He nodded in satisfaction. Yes, that was it.

He had a comfortable life here, and he wanted nothing disturbing it. He and Cully stole an occasional horse from Enoch, when they could find a safely isolated one. There was always a market north across the line. He never tried to drive off a big band; he had no intentions of getting rich overnight. The Parnells would never notice an occasional horse gone. And if they did, they could put it down to so many causes. All natural causes, like wandering off or destroyed by a cougar or wolves. A man never noticed a drop of water now and then. But pelt him with a downpour, and he was soon gasping for relief.

Cully sat in a chair by the door, watching his sister. Linus thought that might be concern in those smoky black eyes. He thought scornfully, Cully didn't have to worry about her. Letty had all the natural equipment to do well by herself.

He said, "Sit down. You make me nervous."

Letty sat down, but her hands were not still. They plucked at her skirt, they fiddled with the neckline of her dress. Women were always fidgety creatures.

Linus asked, "Things going well with the Parnells?" He could depend upon Letty telling him everything that went wrong for them, and he enjoyed hearing about it.

She said sullenly, "All they talk about is losing cattle."

"Ah," Linus said with satisfaction. He had hoped that the drought was squeezing them. He wished he could be around to hear their squeals.

Letty said passionately, "I hope everything goes wrong for them. I hope they're wiped out."

Linus's alarm came back. Something *was* wrong over there. She was a damned fool to make a wish like that. Didn't she see what could happen? If the Parnells were wiped out, Linus could wind up with Letty back on his hands. A daughter was never a profitable thing to a man. She cost him money instead of making him any.

His alarm faded. The Parnells were a good-sized outfit. They might be bent, but they couldn't be broken.

He said, "What kind of fool talk is that? You thinking of enjoying cutting your own throat?"

Cully stirred in his chair. His eyes never left his sister's face.

"I don't care," she said. "You don't know how they treat me. Enoch looks at me like I was dirt. Owen insults me. And Molly makes a slave of me. Nothing I can do can satisfy her." She had an audience, and she was beginning to enjoy this.

Cully's eyes remained fixed on her with a motionless glitter. Far back in them a flame was starting. It dissipated the dead black color. It made his eyes look wicked and hot. He knew what Letty was suffering. The Parnells were like all the others. Mixed blood was something to spit on.

Linus said callously, "You got a husband. Let him protect you."

Letty put her hands over her face. She looked at Cully between her fingers. He believed her.

She said brokenly, "He doesn't care what happens to me. I wish I could make something bad happen to all of them."

Linus laid down in the bunk. "You're not very bright then. What happens to them happens to you. You keep that in mind." He suspected he knew what she was up to. Letty was bored and rode over here with that fool story, hoping to get a sympathetic ear. Let Cully listen to her. He was going back to sleep.

"If you don't care," Letty cried and rushed outside. She knew Cully would follow her. She was three years older than Cully, and she had taken over his care after their mother died. She could always do anything she wanted with Cully.

A hand caught her arm. "I'll stop them," Cully said. His face was wild.

An instant's fright seized her. Maybe she had carried this too far. She didn't care what happened to Linus Derks, but she did care about Cully. If he even made a threat against any of the Parnells, they could shoot him without fear of punishment. But if he harmed one of them, he would be hanged. There was no fairness, where their blood was concerned.

She said earnestly, "No, Cully. There's too many of them." She gave him a wan smile. "I'll go back and do the best I can. If it gets too bad, I'll come back here."

He said harshly, "If it gets too bad, send for me." He had no intention of going against the Parnells personally. There were other ways to hurt them, other ways to occupy their minds and keep them off Letty.

He let the wires down and watched her as she rode away. His hating was an accumulation of all the past abuses—his and hers.

She turned in the saddle to wave to him. Her boredom was quite gone. She smiled as she remembered the anger in Cully's eyes. She could always stir him. She was halfway home before she thought, I didn't take my swim. She didn't need it. The day didn't seem nearly as hot as when she had started out.

Hours later, a lone rider was a black silhouette against the lighter backdrop of the night. He dismounted and struck a match, and its tiny flame was a weak illumination in the immense blackness. Its light showed a pair of eyes, glittering with purpose. The figure stooped and thrust the flame into the dried grass.

The grass caught with a crackling sound. It flared up, then died to a weak red line. It inched across the ground, fanning out a little from its advancing point. The night air was heavy and holding, the wind absent. But the wind would come again in the morning, and its prevailing direction was toward the Parnells. The air would lighten with the sun, and the fire would stir and begin to roar. It would create its own draft and feed upon that draft. It would leap feet, where it now crawled inches.

Cully Derks watched it with satisfaction. The fire would move sluggishly the rest of the night hours. By the time it was discovered in the morning, it would be too big to stop. He lit two dozen fires before he stopped. He looked back along the line and thought several of the fires had died. Then he would see a small, glowing eye, its orangeness unwinking. And as he watched, the eye grew larger.

The Parnells would be busy in the morning. It would be a long time before they had time to think about Letty. He mounted and rode toward the cabin. He was satisfied with his work.

Linus Derks awakened in the morning and yawned. He sniffed for the aroma of coffee and there was none. That damned Cully hadn't started breakfast yet.

He looked about the cabin, and Cully wasn't here. "Cully," he roared.

He heard Cully answer him from outside, and he stepped through the doorway. Cully was looking toward the ridge, and his face was fascinated.

Linus saw the thick plume of black smoke, trailing lazily skyward, and his heart jumped into his throat. A prairie fire was an awesome thing, running for thousands of acres of ground. With a wind pushing it, it could outrun a horse, and it caught and roasted alive the slower-footed animals. If it got too big a start, man could not stop it. Only a broad river or the barren sides of a mountain could halt it. By the size of the smoke this one had its start. His fright subsided as he saw the way the column of smoke was leaning. The wind was pushing it away from them, pushing it toward the Parnells.

He said idly, "Now how did that get started? We haven't had any lightning for weeks."

He looked at Cully's face and saw the truth there. "You started it," he yelled. "Why?"

"For Letty," Cully said simply.

"Why, you Goddamned fool," Linus raged. He slashed Cully across the face with the back of his hand. "You believed what she said. She was enjoying stirring you up. She was putting on a show for you." His mind cast about, seeking an answer in the future. If the Parnells lost a lot of range, they would be forced to move cattle. And the shortest route was through here. Enoch Parnell wouldn't waste a couple of days looking for a new ford. Not when his cattle were hungry. He would come through here, and that fence wouldn't stop him.

Cully said, "I didn't think—"

"Shut up," Linus snapped. There had to be a way he could turn this to profit. If he could take this to court, he might be able to prove that Enoch's cattle had trampled all the crops he had labored to grow. He looked at the spot where the imaginary garden was growing, and he almost knew an honest indignation. A man had rights. The law had to protect those rights. But he would need witnesses. They wouldn't be hard to get. He could collect a half-dozen nesters up and down the creek, nesters who hated the big outfits, nesters who would be glad to swear that Enoch Parnell's cattle trampled Linus Derks' efforts right into the ground. Yes, he could make a profit out of this.

He said, "Saddle my horse. I got some riding to do this morning." He wanted to collect some men, he wanted them here, when Enoch Parnell came.

He watched the smoke while he waited for Cully to bring his horse. The broken teeth showed in a wicked grin. He wished he could be at the Parnells when one of them looked up and discovered the smoke. He wished he could see them running around and hollering.

SIX

Owen came out of the house and scanned the sky. He always looked at the sky the first thing in the morning, hoping to see its steel blueness broken by clouds. This morning was no different from the long succession of mornings. As early as it was, it was hot. The sun was getting that brassy look it would hold until it sank at night. He thought irritably, more of the same hot weather. Day after day of it drained a man's energy until even thinking became an effort.

He shifted his eyes, and it seemed as if a giant hand clamped about his throat, shutting off his breathing and stopping the action of his heart. A great plume of black smoke lifted on a slant toward the sky. The slant showed the direction of the wind. The wind was pushing the smoke toward the Parnells. Owen could not see the fire, but by the volume of the smoke, he knew the fire was a big one. Fear dried his mouth and made his tongue stiff. Any man who had been through a prairie fire knew fear. Broomed by a wind, these fires raced faster than a horse could run. They widened their fronts, moving in a rolling wall of flame higher than a man's head. Black clouds of smoke boiled up from the flames, smoke that could curtain the sky for days. An animal would run ahead of that rolling wall of flame, its heart bursting with effort, until the heat the flames generated reached out and sucked the breath from its lungs. The flames would pass over another body, and the air would reek of charred flesh.

Owen tried again, and his tongue moved. "Enoch! Chad," he bawled.

The urgency in his tone pulled them running from the house. He saw the dismay stamp their faces as they looked at the smoke, holding there as though the expression was sculptured in stone.

"Jesus," Chad said, and it was a prayer and not an oath.

Enoch cursed, breaking his trance. "Les, Hamp," he roared. His eyes cast about, picking his plan of action. The homeplace was directly in line of the fire. If the flames touched these tinder-dry buildings, nothing could save them. Owen saw the brief agony in Enoch's eyes as he made his decision. Nothing could be done for the cattle. They would have to shift for themselves, running ahead of the flames, or finding what poor shelter they could. There would be dead cattle in the fire's wake, cows too old to run fast or far, young calves with little endurance.

Scotty was the first of the four hands out of the bunkhouse. He didn't have to ask questions. He could see the direction in which the Parnells were staring, he could see the smoke.

"Oh, my God," he said hoarsely.

Enoch swore at him, breaking the dumb shock on Scotty's face. "Scotty, you and Hamp stay at the house. Fill everything you can with water."

Owen thought it wasted effort. They could fill every pot and pan in the house, and if the fire touched any of the buildings, all the water they could douse on it would not even slow the flames. Protest would be useless. Enoch would not listen.

"Molly," Enoch yelled.

She came out on the porch, and he stabbed a finger in the direction of the flames. Her eyes widened, and her mouth sagged. She showed no other emotion. Letty stood beside her, her eyes like pieces of black glass. Spittle ran down her chin from a slack mouth. Fear shook her in a great hand, and Owen could see her lips fighting to form words.

"Run," Letty screamed. "It'll burn us all."

She turned to bolt, and Molly seized her arm. She slapped her, and Owen heard the sharp, small report. Letty covered her stinging cheek and whimpered. Her eyes looked nearly normal. The hurt of the blow had cut through the fear.

Molly said crisply, "Go to the well and draw water. I'll bring containers."

Letty moved toward the well, never seeing a step she took. Her eyes were on the smoke.

"Bring me all the matches you've got in the house," Enoch yelled to Molly. "Les, go to the barn and gather up all the gunny bags you can find." He swore as he waited, never realizing he was making a sound.

Enoch distributed the matches and gunny bags. He said, "Spread out and backfire." He and Les and Abel moved beyond the outbuildings, fanning out in a semicircle.

Owen saw Enoch light the first fire, then flail with a gunny bag, beating out the fire's advance. The fire burned sullenly away from him, its progress held back by the strength of the wind. It crawled slowly toward the advancing wall of fire, leaving such a pitifully small burned area behind it.

Les and Abel were doing the same thing. Each fire they lit wanted to travel toward the buildings and not from them. So much time was lost in beating out the persistent, licking tongues of the set fires and forcing them in the right direction. The backfiring was a solid move, if they had the time. Owen didn't think they had the time. The big fire was close enough that he could smell it, and the air was beginning to be charged with its heat. Even if the three men could make a solid half ring of their backfires, they didn't have enough time to burn a swath wide enough to keep the main flames from jumping it.

Chad started to move toward Enoch, and Owen shook his head. "It's too late for backfiring to do any good, Chad."

Enoch straightened from his efforts and glanced toward them. Congested blood, from his furious work, darkened his face. The sooty ashes, puffing up under each flailing blow, were beginning to coat skin and clothes. He stared unbelievingly at his two sons and yelled, "You two get up here."

Chad glanced uneasily at his brother.

Owen said, "We've got one small chance, Chad. Saddle up."

He ran toward the corral and heard the pound of Chad's following feet. This was direct disobedience of Enoch's order, and Enoch would be raving. He grabbed his saddle from the rack and kicked down the bars of the corral. A half-dozen horses were in the corral, and the smell of the fire was driving them crazy. Their eyes rolled, showing mostly white, and their shrill neighing tore at a man's ears. They raced about the corral, their fright keeping them from seeing the opened gate.

Owen roped Major and manhandled him into submission. He heard Chad's swearing as Chad fought the mount he selected. He cinched the saddle, and Major quietened at the familiar touch. The trembling was still in the animal, running down its hide in solid rippling waves.

He mounted, a loop dangling from his hand. Caesar, Enoch's prize yearling, was the smallest animal in the corral. Owen knew a regret as he threw his loop. It settled over Caesar's neck, and he put Major in motion, tugging the yearling after him.

He rode past Enoch toward the roaring line of fire and heard his yell. The wind and his pace split the words into shreds of sound. Owen thought, he'll yell more after it's over.

He rode on an angle toward the southwest. The yearling fought the rope until it choked, then followed. Owen looked back. He was well outside and to the left of the last outbuilding. If he could stop the fire here and continue the line until it extended beyond the buildings on the right-hand side, he might save the homeplace.

He stopped and dismounted. The heat of the flames made his skin dry and itchy. The fire had advanced with unbelievable speed. He could hear its crackling and see the black smoke streaks in the rolling wall of red. He had seen worse prairie fires. This moment would probably be his only grateful one that the grass was short this year. Behind him, Enoch and the two men still worked frantically. Their half circle wasn't a third fired.

Owen looked up at Chad and drew his pistol. He shook his head and shot the yearling between the eyes. It was the only expression of regret he would allow himself. He placed his shot well. Caesar dropped, made one convulsive heave, and was still.

He said, "Throw me your loop."

Chad flipped the rope to him, and Owen placed it about the yearling's rear hoofs. He tightened his own loop about the front hoofs and remounted. The yearling was heavy, but the two horses could drag it. Chad's eyes gleamed as he saw what Owen had in mind. The dragging carcass should smother the line of fire.

Owen nodded and headed toward the fire. They had to use spur and quirt to force the horses toward the flames. Owen pointed across the flames, and Chad sank his spurs deep. His mount bounded through the thin, fiery wall.

Chad rode the windward side, Owen the other. They spurred

their mounts into full speed, dragging the yearling's body over the line of fire. The wind licked tongues of flame at Owen, and the thirty-foot rope was not long enough to keep the heat from him. It seared his throat and shriveled the hairs on the back of his hand.

He looked behind him, and the bouncing carcass blotted out the line of fire. Where leaping flame had been a few seconds ago was now only a blackened line. They raced some five hundred yards before his rope burned through. He threw up his hand, signaling Chad to stop, wheeled Major, and joined Chad on the windward side.

He drew deep on his lungs trying to get the heat and the smell of smoke out of them. The hairs of Major's coat were singed, and a line of blisters was forming on the off foreleg. Major would need doctoring.

Owen's face and hands were black, and his clothes looked as if they would never wash clean. Somewhere in that mad dash he had lost his hat. But the line of fire was broken. It swept forward at the two ends, but the house and buildings sat in an oasis of unburned grass. Enoch and the others should be able to handle any fire that licked out from the sides.

Owen put a brief glance on the dead yearling. A few moments ago that charred, raw mass of flesh had been a promising colt.

He said, "We'd better check for sparks."

They rode the blackened line, dismounting to stomp out a spot fire or a spark. The main fire was beyond the buildings, its two tongues swerving to join up again.

"He'll raise hell," Chad said gloomily.

Owen nodded without speaking. That went without saying.

They rode slowly toward the waiting people. It had been close. The fire had passed within thirty yards of one of the barns. Molly's eyes were shining as she watched her sons dismount.

Hamp and Abel and the others looked at each other and grinned. The buildings were saved, and the relief was in those grins. Only Enoch's face remained harsh.

Owen handed Major's reins to Scotty and said, "Doctor him, will you, Scotty? He got burned."

Scotty ran his hand over the animal's neck. "He'll get the best."

Enoch breathed hard, as he glared at Owen. "Did you have to take Caesar?"

Owen's voice was weary as he pointed out the obvious. "The older horses were too heavy to drag."

Molly's face was furious as she looked at her husband. "You should be grateful. He saved the buildings." The men stared uneasily at the ground, and Molly checked a further outbreak.

She said, "Come on, Letty. There's ashes over everything. We won't get through cleaning up today."

Owen walked toward the well, feeling a dull resentment. He was foolish to expect Enoch's approval. He hadn't won it in anything, yet.

SEVEN

The fire burned out at the river, leaving an ashy waste behind it. The Parnell buildings were an island in a sea of black ruin. The burrowing animals escaped, and when the earth cooled sufficiently, they came out to face starvation. The grass-eating animals and the predators faced the same problem. Unless they could escape this vast black emptiness, both would die.

Grass ash was light. Each puff of wind stirred it, each footstep blew a cloud upward about a man's face. The smoke still lingered and combined with the drifting ash, it hung a gray curtain in the air, dulling the sun until it was only a faint orb in the sky.

Enoch did not have to tell his hands, or his sons to saddle. Each man knew the emergency they faced. Unless a quick gather was made and the cattle driven onto unburned range, they would wander aimlessly, bawling for something to eat. The light ash, puffing upward at every step, would fill their eyes and nostrils, and they would go mad under the twin scourge of thirst and hunger. This range could be forgotten until next year. The spring rains would bring new grass. It would be greener than before, but it would lack nourishment, for the moisture-retaining mulch was burned, and the new grass would not be as hardy.

Enoch cinched his saddle and stared bleakly at the blackened acres. "I should have killed Derks the day he moved in. He started this fire."

The fire came from Derks' direction. It was likely it was set by human agency, for there had been no lightning strikes for weeks. Did Derks' animosity toward Enoch extend to the length of setting fires? Owen admitted the possibility. If he knew for sure, he would have no feeling about shooting Derks, himself. But there was no proof. And you couldn't shoot a man because you had a strong suspicion against him.

Enoch said savagely, "By God, he'll pay for Caesar and everything else."

Owen said curtly, "Move against him, and you'll have Kilmonte on your neck. You've got no proof Derks did it."

Opposition always brought out the wicked fire in Enoch's eyes. "Are you saying Derks wouldn't do it?"

Owen's face was dispassionate as he swung into the saddle. It was useless trying to reason with Enoch. He said, "We've got work to do."

He rode off without looking back. Enoch would not drop his suspicions of Derks. He would let them lay in his mind until their festering demanded action. The action could bring a lot of harm to the E-P. You stubborn, old fool, Owen thought, with a burst of anger. They had some bad days ahead of them, bad enough without Enoch making them worse.

It took two days to make the gather. Men were in the saddle before the light strengthened in the east, and darkness caught them before they dismounted. They would stagger stiffly for several steps until the hinges of their knees unlocked, eat a few hurried bites, then fall into the sodden oblivion of sleep.

They found losses, and the glitter in Enoch's eyes grew more pronounced with each discovery. The losses were mostly young calves and old cows, fallen where the heated air sucked the air from their lungs. The young and the old always went first.

Riders combed coulees and draws, driving the protesting animals ahead of them. It was a hasty combing, and the individuals, the strays had to be left behind. They would wander about in the ashes, their bawling growing weaker as their hunger increased. A man shut his mind to them. He concentrated upon saving the bulk of the herd.

It was hard to keep the herd under control. Their thirst and their hunger kept the cattle milling restlessly at night, and their bawling was constant. It would grow much worse before it bettered. Owen figured they had at least a four-day drive before they reached fresh range. In four days, this herd would be maddened, ready to bolt on the slightest pretext. A whiff of water, so far away that man could not detect it, would send them in wild flight. Riders had to be alert to catch the first sign of stampede, and if they could not check it, they had to be sure the stampede was headed in the right direction. If it wasn't, countless miles would be lost, and those miles could be the difference.

Owen looked at the faces ringed about Enoch. Last night had been a sleepless one, and men were red-eyed. Their faces were black except for the white circles of their eyes and the thin, white line around their lips. All night the shuffling hoofs of the cattle raised the weightless, sooty ash. A man grew coated with it. He breathed it, he ate it. Water could not wash the taste of it from his mouth.

Enoch ran his tongue around his lips and spat on the ground. "We're driving to Larkin's crossing." He said it to all of them, but his eyes were on Owen. Larkin was gone, but to Enoch, it was still Larkin's crossing.

Owen thought of the fence Derks had stretched. He remembered the hate flowing between Derks and his father. It would be a waste of time driving to that fence. Derks wouldn't let them through.

"Derks won't let you cross," Owen said flatly.

"He'll let us," Enoch said. With his soot-blackened face and his red-rimmed eyes he looked as if he were in the wrong layer of the world. "He'll let us cross," he repeated. "Or I'll tear down his damned fence."

Owen said slowly, "He might choose to fight you." If Derks did, Kilmonte and the law were on his side.

Enoch raked him with a cutting glance. "You worry about it." He lifted his voice. "Move 'em out."

They got the herd strung out in the semblance of a drive. The drag and flank men had some busy moments, for the cattle kept trying to break back to familiar range, and it took hard riding to turn them. Owen cursed the soot that billowed up around him, and he heard the others curse it with the same feeling.

It was going to be a hard drive, with another dry camp in

store for the night. Tomorrow night would be the fourth day without food or water for the cattle. They would be maddened and almost impossible to hold. Maybe Enoch was taking the only course open by driving to Larkin's crossing.

The cattle shuffled through miles of ashes, each hoof impact against the earth adding more of the weightless dust to the air. It was like riding through a blackish fog. The stuff coated flesh and added new layers, and a man's skin itched and stung under it.

This was Owen's first experience on a drive after a prairie fire, but he had heard the old timers talk about it. He had listened to them with a hidden grin, thinking they were putting it on, trying to impress him. He apologized to those old timers. They hadn't been able to describe the misery at all. By noon, a man thought he was riding through hell. The sun poured down through the murky grayness, and the air was so hot it dizzied the senses. Owen could feel the skin on his hands cracking and burning from the dryness. The neckscarf gave a little protection to his face below the eyes. He wished he could spit, and he couldn't raise a drop of moisture. The misery dulled his senses, and he wanted to sleep. He cursed to dispell the drowsiness, and the sound of his voice startled him. It came out hoarse and croaking. He straightened his aching back and blinked several times. He had to keep his attention on the herd. He had to watch his horse, too. Madness could touch it as well as the cattle.

"Hey, Owen."

The voice startled him, and he twisted in the saddle. Chad rode up out of the murk. His scarf masked him to the eyes. With the black expanse above it, he looked like a bandit hunting for work.

Chad's voice was muffled by the scarf. He tried to be casual, but he couldn't keep the trembling out of it. "My eyes got to aching so bad I was seeing double."

Owen nodded. A man peered through the murk and the baking heat until it felt as though red-hot wires were pulling his eyeballs from his head.

Chad's attempt at a laugh didn't come off. "I got to thinking I was the only man left in this dirty world. Just me and a bunch of filthy cows to herd. I had to ride up to see if you were still here." He was ashamed of his outbreak, and he tried to make his voice indifferent. "Think we'll make it?"

"We'll make it." Owen knew how Chad felt. A man's misery

grew so great that it wasn't hard to imagine he was completely alone, that there wasn't another person in the world to help him.

"What if Derks won't let us through?"

"Then we'll run over him." Owen tried to grin, and it hurt his cracked lips. He was reversing his stand of the morning, when he had argued against Enoch saying the same thing. But things were different, too. They didn't have another two days to drive to another ford. Tomorrow would be stretching them pretty thin.

Chad said somberly, "He's right again, isn't he?"

Owen nodded. Enoch was always right. Chad was younger and more rebellious. Owen thought, it probably galls him more than it does me.

"Chad," Enoch yelled.

Chad jerked his head. He couldn't see his father.

"Watch that Goddamned white steer," Enoch roared. "He's throwing his head."

Chad muttered, "He doesn't miss a damned thing," and dropped back.

Owen watched the mass of bobbing heads, moving in rhythm to the slow, plodding walk. The old man was tough. He was as miserable as any of them, yet his attention never wavered. He had seen that white steer throwing its head, readying for a break. Yes, they would get through. Enoch Parnell would see to it.

They drove deep into the night. The cattle stumbled with weariness, and the horses were in little better shape. A man rode slumped in his saddle, fragments of thought swirling in his head. It was hard to get a hold of a complete thought. How much of this does he think we can stand, Owen thought. He was too worn to even curse, and he heard no cursing from the other riders. It was a dangerous quietness. A man swore to relieve boredom and minor discomfort. When he became sullenly quiet, he was at the breaking point.

Laggard animals had been dropping for the past two hours. Enoch would not let a rider stop beside a fallen cow. "Let it be," he yelled. A rider could waste precious minutes trying to get the weakened animal back on its feet. There was no time to save the individual. Only the bulk of the herd was to be considered.

They stopped shortly before midnight. Owen almost fell out of the saddle, and he had to grab the horn to hold himself erect.

Enoch came toward him, his steps heavy, but he was still moving.

He said, "Get Chad and see that the herd is bedded down. I'll send someone out to relieve you in a couple of hours."

Bitter protest filled Owen's mouth, and he swallowed hard against its escape. Enoch was right. One of the men shouldn't be asked to do something before a Parnell did it.

Enoch said, "We ought to reach McDonald's creek shortly after noon tomorrow."

It was a statement of fact and not encouragement. But Enoch was wise in driving this late tonight. It could cut a half day from tomorrow's drive. The morning heat would be bad enough. The afternoon's heat was far worse.

He found Chad just ready to unsaddle. He said, "Leave it on. Enoch just gave us first watch."

Chad cursed Enoch with terrible intensity. Owen waited for him to run down and asked, "Do you want me to get one of the men?"

That rasped Chad's pride. "No, Goddamn it. But what does he expect? Isn't there any limit?"

Owen shrugged. Enoch expected to get the herd through. He would drive every man of them until they dropped and not consider the cost too high.

Most of the herd were already down, dropping where Enoch let it stop. Here and there, a cow still stood, her head drooping. Some of them bawled before they sank to the ground. Owen heard the thud as their bodies hit the ground. The black dust rose above them. It was going to be hard to get them up in the morning. Once a cowbrute thought she was through, nothing could make her get on her feet again.

He began the slow, monotonous circle of the bedding ground. Lead weights were attached to his eyelids, dragging them shut. Two hours was the longest stretch of time invented by man.

They had trouble getting the herd started in the morning. Some of the animals had to be tailed up. The herd strung out in a weary, shuffling line. Owen heard very little bawling. That was bad. When cattle stopped bawling, they were on the verge of quitting. Once the thought was fully anchored, they would stop. And three times the number of riders couldn't force them on.

His horse plodded through the morning hours. A rider could let his thoughts wander, for there wasn't the strength left in the cattle to bolt. Enoch's wisdom in driving late last night was evident. This herd couldn't make it through another long afternoon.

Enoch called Owen's name twice before Owen realized he was near.

Enoch said impatiently, "We're only a couple of miles from the creek. I'm holding the herd here. I want to talk to Derks."

Owen looked at the herd. Two miles might not be enough. Some of the animals were lifting their heads. If they got the water smell, they would come on a dead run.

Enoch growled, "Are you coming with me?"

Owen could point out that Enoch hadn't asked him. He lifted his reins. He wanted to be along. It sounded as though Enoch intended to negotiate with Derks for a crossing. Enoch must be growing soft. The thought gave Owen wry amusement.

They passed out of the burned area a half mile before they reached the fence. Owen saw Enoch's eyes blaze as he looked at the unburned grass. Long fingers of black reached back into the grass, showing where the fire had died out against the wind. Owen would say someone had gone along here setting individual fires. His say was poor proof.

Derks and Cully were waiting for them at the fence. Five men stood behind them, their faces anxious. Owen knew Benton and Dougan. He could not recall the others' names. All of them were little nesters, strung up and down the creek. Nesters were transient people, moving with the good and bad years. A man couldn't keep up with them.

He thought, they're going to make a fight of it. But he saw no guns, and the impression didn't square with the anxiety on their faces.

Enoch rode up to the group and stared impassively down at Linus Derks. Derks squirmed under the weight of the appraisal.

Enoch said, "If I find out you set that fire, I'll kill you."

Derks' voice went shrill. "By God, you got no right to ride up here and threaten me. I've got witnesses."

Owen felt a terrible temptation to smash that face. He said, "Shut up."

Enoch flashed him a glance. Owen couldn't tell if it held surprise or approval.

"We're crossing here," Enoch said. "Take down those wires."

"I won't," Derks shouted. "A man's got rights. I won't have your cattle trampling my place, ruining my garden." A look of cupidity squeezed his eyes. "If you're willing to pay for damages, I might consider it. I'd say two hundred dollars is about right."

Derks didn't have a garden. He had water and a little grass. At the moment, those were valuable commodities but not two hundred dollars' worth.

Owen started to yell his outrage, and he heard a noise. He turned his head. The noise sounded like distant thunder except that it was a continuous, rolling sound. It couldn't be thunder for there wasn't a cloud in the sky. A stampeding herd made that kind of rumble. It was part noise and part vibration, a vibration that traveled through the earth. The herd had smelled water.

He looked at Enoch and said, "They're coming."

Enoch's eyes held some kind of savage pleasure.

Owen thought, maybe he planned it this way. Maybe he drove close enough to be sure the herd would smell water.

Enoch leaned forward and said softly, "Linus, I'd sure as hell get out of the way. And I'd take my witnesses with me."

He jerked his head at Owen and spurred along the fence. Owen followed him. They rode well off to one side before they stopped. The rumble grew louder, and the leaders of the herd appeared on the crest of the slope. Riders rode on either side of them, shouting at the thirst-crazed beasts. They didn't seem to be making too much of an attempt to turn them.

Linus Derks stared openmouthed at the approaching cattle.

Owen thought: if he thinks that fence will turn them, he's crazy. The lead animals might attempt to veer, when they saw it, but the press of the cattle behind them would carry them on through it.

Derks and his group were directly in the herd's path. Owen thought they were going to stand there. If they did, the cattle would trample them under.

Derks broke his trance with a shrill squawk and ran. Cully and the witnesses followed him.

The cattle poured down the slope in a mighty wave. The leaders hit the wire, and Owen saw posts jerked out of the ground. He imagined he could hear the sharp twangs as wires broke. They would have cut cattle on their hands, perhaps cut badly enough to destroy.

A dozen sections of the fence were down, and the cattle poured through, heading on the most direct line for the creek. Owen thought they were going to run through the house, and at the last split second, the wave split and passed around it. The shed wasn't as fortunate. It was a flimsy structure on pole supports. One of the animals brushed a pole and carried it away. The shed roof tilted, then slid out of view under the smashing hoofs. In a space of a breath, the shed was kindling.

The cattle waded into the water up to their bellies, and their thirsty sucking of it was a distinct sound. The water washed soot from their legs and bellies, and the water below them flowed black.

They came out of the creek, their sunken bellies swollen tight with water. They fell hungrily on the green grass along the creek's edge.

Derks ran at them trying to drive them from the grass. For a lone man on foot, it was a hopeless task. Some of the cattle didn't even raise their heads at his screaming voice and waving arms. Others moved a few steps, then fell to again.

Sweat washed Derks' features, and his face was red with exertion. He stopped and panted. Enoch was flanked by his sons and riders. All of them were grinning, their teeth gleaming in black faces.

"I'll show you," Derks yelled. "You can't smash up my property and eat up my horses' grass. You'll see. We got some law here."

Enoch sat and gave him that cold, wolfish grin.

EIGHT

The fire forced the drive to summer range two weeks earlier than usual, but the upper range was sufficient to carry the herd.

Owen tried to talk to Chad about his concern for the fall. They needed heavy rains to bring back the grass on the lower ranges.

Chad was not interested. They had been up in the mountains for over a week, and his thoughts were of Letty. "How much longer are we going to sit around here?" he asked sulkily. "He's got Scotty and Hamp and the others to look after the herd. That's what he hires them for."

Owen knew why Enoch was staying. It hurt a cattleman to see his cattle gaunted. And it did his heart good to see the beasts on adequate feed. When a cow had enough grass to stuff her belly full, she could recover flesh in an amazingly short time. Already, the cattle were beginning to put on a little weight.

Chad stared moodily at Scotty. Scotty squatted beside the fire, stirring something in a pot. "I don't know what he's cooking," Chad said. "But you can bet it's got venison in it."

They had made the gather and drive in such a hurry there was no time to bring necessary provisions. Their diet for the past week had been mostly venison. Owen grinned at the sourness in Chad's voice. He was sick of deer meat, himself.

He saw Enoch moving toward them and cautioned, "Don't let him hear you complaining. He'll keep you up here." He saw the tight look appear around Chad's mouth. Chad feared the prospect. He wanted to get back to Letty.

Enoch frowned at his sprawled-out sons. He detested idleness, even when there was nothing to do. A man could loaf away hours up here, for the cattle would not stray from this valley with its ample grass.

Chad yawned and stretched. "It's nice up here. I'd like to stay the summer."

Owen saw Enoch make his snap decision. "We're going back today," Enoch said. "I'm leaving Hamp and Scotty. We've got plenty of work to do below." He put a final disapproving glance on them. "We'll leave in the next hour."

Chad's eyes sparkled, when Enoch left them.

Owen shook his head. "You're getting as sneaky as an Indian."

He saw Chad's eyes go cold. He had meant no reference to Letty. Apology would only make it worse. A man had to watch his tongue all the time.

Owen looked back as they left the camp. Hamp and Scotty were grinning. They would be on their backs before Enoch was out of sight. Owen didn't envy them. The big Fourth of July celebration and dance was in town next week. He wanted to get back and take Evlalie to it.

They stopped at the spring in the foothills. It flowed out of the hill and formed a large pool before it trickled off and lost itself. The horses would get no more water until they reached McDonald's creek. The dry weather was affecting the spring. The pool wasn't nearly as large as it had been last year.

Owen thought Enoch might find another crossing, but his father headed straight for Derks' place.

"That fence will still be down," Enoch said. "He only put it up to bother me."

Enoch was right about the fence. Derks hadn't touched it. The posts were still out of the ground, or leaning crazily, and the wire was a tangled mess. The little cavalcade of riders passed close to Derks' house. Derks stood in the doorway, watching them. He did not move or attempt to hail them. But he wasn't ignoring them. Owen caught the triumphant set of the man's face. Derks was pleased about something.

They rode back across the burned area. The wind had broomed away most of the ash, but the blackness remained. Enoch's face was harsh as he rode through it. He wasn't forgetting.

A roan gelding was tied in front of the house. Enoch said, "That's Kilmonte's horse. What's he doing here?"

Owen shook his head. He had a quick uneasiness. Was Kilmonte's being here and the triumph in Derks' face tied in together?

Molly came out to the corral, while they were unsaddling. "Enoch," she said. "The sheriff's here."

"I got eyes," Enoch growled.

She gave him an exasperated glance. "He's been here every day for the last three days. He has a—" She stopped as she saw Kilmonte coming toward them.

Chad had no curiosity about Kilmonte's presence. He stripped his gear from his horse, turned the animal into the corral, and headed for the house, looking for Letty.

Kilmonte's face was grave as he looked at them. "Enoch. Owen," he said.

Les and Abel discreetly withdrew. This was the boss's business.

Enoch returned the greeting with a curt nod. He let Kilmonte do the talking.

Kilmonte said, "I've got a subpoena to serve on you. Linus Derks is suing you."

Enoch's face showed his astonishment. "For what?"

"For the damages you did his place, when you drove over it."

"Why Goddamn him," Enoch exploded. "What damages could I do his place?"

The familiar, stubborn set hardened Kilmonte's face. "I'm not here to argue with you." He handed a paper to Enoch. "You be in court in the morning." His eyes bored into Enoch. "Or I'll be back with a warrant for your arrest." He turned and strode away. Enoch raved and cursed at him. Kilmonte didn't turn his head.

It was a bad afternoon and evening. Owen wanted to ride over to the Denton's. He wanted to ask Evlalie to go to that dance. He couldn't get away from Enoch. He sat and listened to

Enoch curse Derks and Kilmonte for the hundredth time. He thought gloomily, Chad was the lucky one. Chad was locked in that room with Letty.

Two dozen spectators were in the courtroom, when Enoch and Owen walked into it. Most of them were nesters, and Owen doubted there was a man in the room who liked Enoch. Enoch hadn't brought Chad. "We don't need him," he said. "He'd be useless, anyway. His head's filled with that woman."

We might need everyone we can get, Owen thought. Judge Brisbaine would hear the case. He sat at his bench, his jowls overflowing his collar. He was a little man with a pugnacious cut to his jaw. His authority let him exercise that pugnaciousness.

He looked at the clock and snapped, "You're late."

Enoch was, by twenty minutes. He snorted, "I've got other things to do than to spend my time on this damned nonsense."

The red flowed up from Brisbaine's collar.

Oh God, Owen groaned silently. Stir him up. Stir him up real good.

Derks had hired a lawyer. He sat at a table with Luther Selvy. He tried to keep his face grave, but a grin kept twitching at his lip corners.

Owen thought, he's sure of himself. He distrusted Selvy. Selvy was a smooth, polished man, but his eyes had a lean, hungry look. Perhaps he was being unfair to Selvy. But he had a natural distrust of all lawyers. Every time a man got mixed up with one, it cost him.

Derks' five witnesses sat in the first row of chairs, behind him. They stared at the floor. Derks was well-armed. Against Derks' preparation, Enoch had his temper.

Judge Brisbaine said sarcastically, "Now, if Mr. Parnell doesn't mind, we'll get started."

Enoch glowered at him.

You're doing fine, Owen thought. Before you even open your mouth, you're losing it.

Selvy put Derks on the stand. Derks made a good impression. He was cleaner than Owen had ever seen him, and he answered respectfully.

Selvy said, "Tell the judge what happened."

Derks sighed. He hated to do this to Enoch. "Judge, I got just a little place. I want to be neighborly. But I've got to think of myself, too. I put up a fence to protect what little grass I have.

All those cattle would have eaten me out in a couple hours' time. When my grass is gone, I can't go someplace else." His look at Enoch said, he's got the whole country.

Brisbaine nodded sympathetically.

Derks isn't this clever, Owen thought furiously. Those had to be Selvy's words coming out of Derks' mouth. He was building himself up as a little man against a big, ruthless neighbor. Maybe the picture wasn't too far off, Owen admitted, but Derks was giving it a twist that was all wrong. He heard choking sounds deep in Enoch's throat. Owen touched his arm, trying to calm him, and Enoch glared at him.

"Go on," Selvy said.

"I wasn't shutting him out from his summer range," Derks said. "There's other crossings. But he insisted he had to come across my place. I figured up the damage the cattle would do and set him a fair price. He wouldn't listen to me. He pushed his cattle through my fence, and I lost my grass and my garden."

"He's a damned liar," Enoch shouted. "He tried to hold me up. He only built that fence to—"

Brisbaine banged on the bench. His face was choleric. "Another outbreak like that, and I'll hold you in contempt."

Enoch stared wildly, but he subsided.

Selvy asked, "How much do you figure you lost, Mr. Derks?"

Derks looked at the floor as though Enoch's outbreak had frightened him.

"Tell the judge," Selvy said.

"Well, all my grass is gone. And my garden is gone. I lost a shed. Smashed all to pieces. And part of my fence. I was figuring getting me a few steers to put on that grass." His face was hopeless. "I can't, now."

"You were depending on that garden and those steers for food?"

"I was." Derks sighed. "Cully and me will just have to make out some other way."

Enoch was ready to yell again, and Owen's fingers bit into his arm. He didn't care how much Enoch glared. He said in a low voice, "You'll get your chance."

"How much do you figure all this damage cost you?" Selvy asked.

Derks looked at Brisbaine. "I figure it comes close to three hundred dollars. I'm a poor man, sir. If we have a bad winter—" He shook his head and did not finish.

Selvy said, "That will be all, Mr. Derks."

Derks moved back to the table. A secret, wicked laughter was just below the surface. Owen thought he would burst, trying to hold it. Three hundred dollars! It was a ridiculous figure. When Enoch heard it, Owen was sure the blood was going to break through his face.

He said, "Easy," and retained his grip on Enoch's arm.

Selvy called Cully and the five witnesses to the stand. They corroborated Derks' story. The five witnesses said they had been visiting Derks and had heard him plead with Parnell not to destroy his fence. Benton pointed to Enoch and said, "Then he drove his cattle right over the fence. We had to run for our lives."

Enoch yelled, "He's a liar," and jumped to his feet. Owen tugged at him, and Enoch threw off his hand. "Nothing's been said about that fire being set. Nothing's been said about my range being burned out."

Brisbaine was furious. He pounded like an insane man. "Order," he shouted. "Order."

Selvy said silkily, "Your Honor, let Mr. Parnell take the stand. Perhaps we haven't heard all of this."

Brisbaine stabbed a finger at Enoch. "One more outbreak, and I'll fine you."

Oh, God, Owen groaned. Selvy will tie him in knots.

Selvy waited until Enoch was seated, then said, "Tell us about that fire, Mr. Parnell."

Owen could hear the sound of Enoch's breathing. Enoch was making a tremendous effort to control himself. "Somebody set a fire," he said. "It burned my range. It almost got my house and buildings. We had to make a fast drive." His eyes burned at Selvy. "My cattle were without food or water for four days by the time we got to that fence. Finding another crossing would have taken another two days. We didn't have the time."

"But the cattle are all right now," Selvy said. "They did make it. You can swear they couldn't have gone another two days?"

Enoch's temper was rising again. Being a reasonable man wasn't doing any good. "I can swear it," he shouted.

Selvy murmured, "No man can say how much an animal can endure. You said somebody set that fire? Are you accusing Mr. Derks?"

Enoch was shaking with anger, but he had enough sense left not to fall into that trap. "I've got no proof," he said sullenly. "But it was set."

"Could you be blaming Mr. Derks for an act of God? Couldn't lightning have caused the fire?"

"We haven't had any lightning in weeks," Enoch yelled.

"But in your mind you accuse Mr. Derks of lighting a fire. And in retaliation you drove your cattle across his land."

"Goddamn it. You're twisting it," Enoch roared.

Brisbaine said icily, "That will cost you twenty-five dollars, Mr. Parnell. Keep on, and you'll make it more."

Enoch glared wildly about the room. Kilmonte stood in the rear of the room, watching intently. Owen knew how Enoch felt. Enoch was an old bull at bay before a pack of wolves. Every-way he turned, one of them was ready to leap on him.

Enoch opened his mouth, and Selvy said, "That will be all, Mr. Parnell."

Owen saw a sagging at the corners of Enoch's mouth. Perhaps for the first time, Enoch realized how helpless he was. He stepped down, shaking his head, and the gesture was bewildered. He was up against the law, and the law took the parts of the story it wanted and threw away the rest.

"Owen Parnell," Selvy said.

Owen took a deep breath. Enoch had made a bad witness. If Owen kept his head perhaps he could undo some of the damage Enoch had done.

His voice was calm. "We had to drive to grass and water. We stopped the herd a good two miles from the fence. My father tried to pay for crossing Derks' land. Derks asked two hundred dollars." He wished there were some cattlemen in the room. They would know how ridiculous that price was.

Selvy said, "But that two miles wasn't far enough away to prevent them from getting the smell of water, was it?"

"I guess not," Owen said reluctantly.

A sardonic smile played on Selvy's lips. "You drove them that close, knowing that once they smelled water nothing could stop them. You figured no one could blame you."

"No," Owen said hotly. Selvy could twist things until they sounded altogether different.

Selvy said, "I can tell from your tone you think two hundred dollars is outrageous. Will it replace the grass your cattle ate? The garden they destroyed?"

Owen's face congested with angry blood. "I doubt there was a garden. I didn't see one."

"Are you saying seven men lied? Wouldn't a herd of cattle

trample out a garden until nothing remained?"

Owen said heatedly, "It's damned funny to me that those men happened to be there just waiting for us to show up."

Selvy smiled sadly. "You're not saying a man's friends haven't a right to visit him?"

Owen made a desperate effort to control his temper. He wasn't doing any better than Enoch had. He said, "If that fence was so important to Derks, why wasn't it all around his place? Why was it only built on one side, shutting us off from the ford?"

"It takes time and money to build a fence," Selvy pointed out. "As a cattleman you know that. Mr. Derks isn't as wealthy as some of his neighbors. Isn't it possible that he ran out of both time and money?"

Selvy started to turn away, and Owen protested, "Just a minute."

Selvy looked at Judge Brisbaine and shrugged. "Does Your Honor need to hear more?"

"It would be a waste of this court's time and patience. That will be all," Brisbaine said to Owen.

"No," Owen said. He had to adjust this one-sided picture; he had to make the court look at it from a different view.

"Step down," Brisbaine thundered at him. "Or do you want to be fined for contempt?"

Owen's resistance sagged. It wouldn't do a bit of good for him to be fined. He moved to his father and sat down. His face was white and flinty hard. They had taken quite a licking, and they were helpless to strike one blow in return.

Brisbaine said, "Enoch and Owen Parnell stand up."

He lectured them for fifteen minutes on the responsibility of a man to his neighbor, about the rights of the individual, no matter how small he was. His words were hailstones, bouncing off them.

Owen thought, if he doesn't shut up, Enoch will drag him off that bench.

Brisbaine said, "The law has come to Montana to stay. Because a man has thousands of head of cattle doesn't make him big enough to administer the law as he sees fit. The sooner you learn it, the better off you will be. This court finds for the claimant. You will pay him damages in the amount of three hundred dollars. Sheriff"—Brisbaine looked toward the back of the room—"they will pay these damages before they leave town.

If they try to leave without paying, I'll issue a warrant for their arrest." He banged his gavel. "Court dismissed." He climbed down from his bench and waddled from the room.

Owen thought his father was going to charge the judge. He grabbed his shoulder and hustled him from the room.

Kilmonte followed them out onto the walk. He said heavily, "You'd better go to the bank, Enoch."

Owen looked at those troubled eyes. "Do you claim that was a fair trial?"

"That part of it isn't my job," Kilmonte said. "It was judged on the facts."

"Is that the way you would have judged it, John?"

Kilmonte shook his head, dogged persistence in the gesture. "I don't do any judging."

Enoch found his tongue. He cursed Selvy and Brisbaine. He cursed Kilmonte.

Dull color burned Kilmonte's cheeks. His eyes turned wicked and bright, but he stood there and took it. Owen forgave him a lot in that moment.

Kilmonte said, "Don't force me any more, Enoch."

Owen said, "He didn't have anything to do with what happened in there, Enoch."

Enoch cursed him, and Owen's temper snapped. "Let's pay it and get it over with."

Selvy's appearance saved Owen a further lashing. The lawyer's face went white and tense at the sight of the violence in Enoch's face. But Kilmonte was there. Kilmonte wouldn't let anything happen.

Selvy moved to the edge of the walk, and his stride lengthened. He kept his eyes on his boots.

"Lawyer," Enoch said. A man couldn't put more contempt into a single word. "Lawyer," he repeated. "I'd stay in town, if I were you. I'd make damned sure our paths never crossed again."

Selvy flashed a glance at him, then at Kilmonte. He never spoke or broke his stride.

Kilmonte's thin restraint snapped. "The day's over when you can threaten people as you please. There's laws—"

"Tell me about the law," Enoch said, with wicked softness. "Tell me how your law brought in lice like Selvy. How much did Derks have to give him? How much did he give you?"

Kilmonte breathed like a man after a hard run. When he

spoke, his voice shook with passion. "That's the last thing I'm taking from you, Enoch. Get that money, or I'll get that warrant."

They stood there, glaring at each other, all control gone. Any second, Owen thought, and Enoch will swing at him. Then there will be more hell to pay. He started to step between them, to force them back. Derks and Cully and the five witnesses came out onto the walk. It was a welcome distraction. The five men crowded around Derks, congratulating him.

Derks said, "The drinks are on me, boys. I told you there were laws to protect little men like us."

Enoch forgot about Kilmonte. He moved three strides and clamped a hand on Derks' shoulder. "Linus, some day I'm going to have to kill you." He said it almost conversationally.

Derks squalled. "You heard him, sheriff. You heard him threaten me."

"By God," Kilmonte said furiously. "That's enough." He started to move after Enoch, and Owen caught his arm.

"He's going, John. He's going straight to the bank."

For a moment, he thought he couldn't turn Kilmonte. Then Kilmonte said, "Right now. If he hesitates or takes one step out of the way, I'll throw his ass in jail."

Owen thought grimly, Enoch was going. Enoch didn't have any other choice.

He gripped Enoch's arm and said, "Let's go." They went down the walk together, Owen holding his father's arm. He heard Kilmonte's heavy footsteps following them. Enoch would grow more furious with each passing hour. It would take time for him to realize the full extent of his licking.

NINE

As Owen edged toward the door he heard Molly say wearily, "Yes, you told me, Enoch. I've heard what happened in that courtroom a hundred times."

Owen eased the door shut behind him. The following silence said Molly must have shocked Enoch.

Poor Molly. Owen knew what she was going through. He had heard it almost as often as Molly said she had. All afternoon, he had listened to Enoch raving about it. It was the only subject during suppertime. Owen shook his head. Enoch would belabor the topic for the next two weeks.

He saddled his horse and led it out of the corral. He heard Enoch bawl, "Owen, where are you? I want to talk to you."

Owen mounted and spurred his horse into a run. He was going to ask Evlalie to go to the Fourth of July dance. He wasn't going to sit around all evening and listen to Enoch rave about what had happened this morning.

When he was out of earshot, he eased the horse's pace. The reins rasped against the warts on the inside of the index finger of his left hand. The warts seemed to catch on something with every motion he made. When he returned home, he was going to burn them off with acid.

Denton was on his front porch, when Owen arrived. He was eager to talk about what had happened in town this morning.

Owen sighed. News traveled fast. Everyone within a radius of fifty miles would have heard about it by now. The homesteaders would be gleeful, the cattlemen resentful.

Denton talked about it for twenty minutes. Twice, Owen saw Evlalie come to the door and glance out at them. The darkness obscured her features, but Owen could sense her displeasure.

"It's a damned outrage," Denton said gloomily. "It was legalized robbery, and Brisbaine let it happen. What was Kilmonte doing? I thought we could depend on him."

Owen said, "He didn't have anything to do with the trial, Tom. He had to serve the paper and bring us in. From then on, it was out of his hands."

Denton's shaking head said he wasn't convinced. "It's a hell of a thing, when a man can get no protection from the law."

If Owen would let him, Denton would talk all night on the subject. He said curtly, "We did start it, Tom. We crossed Derks' land."

Denton stared at him in astonishment. "Are you siding with Derks?"

Owen stood. "No." Derks was a cleverer man than he had realized. "I'm just saying we put ourselves in a place where Derks could get at us." He moved toward the door. "I've got to talk to Evlalie." He heard Denton's grumbling. Tom Denton and Enoch should be spending this evening together.

Evlalie answered his knock, and there was a coldness in her face. He wanted to put his arms about her, and he knew better. Her attitude showed nothing but rebuff.

He asked, "Ev, what time shall I pick you up Saturday?"

Sunshine striking off ice had the same cold sheen as her eyes. "For what?"

He frowned. She knew for what. The Fourth of July celebration was something everyone looked forward to.

He thought, don't you give me trouble, Evlalie. I've had about enough trouble for today. "You know what I'm talking about. The celebration and dance."

He knew that look. Her eyes always flecked when she was angry.

"Aren't you giving me too much time?" she asked. "Asking me this far in advance?"

His face showed honest bewilderment. "Good God, Evlalie. You know about the fire. You know I've been busy. I was coming over this morning, but we had to go to town."

The frost extended to her tongue. "I didn't want to interfere with your busy schedule. I was sure you had something more important to do Saturday. Clell Sawtelle asked me a week ago. I accepted."

Anger put a trembling in his body. She knew he was going to ask her. Hadn't they gone together to it last year and the year before. He wished Sawtelle was here. He wanted to knock that idiotic smile off his face.

He said, "You do as you damned please," and whirled for the door.

"I will," she called after him. He had never heard her voice so sharp. "I will," she repeated.

He resisted the impulse to slam the door.

Denton said, "That was short." He looked at Owen and grinned. "Oh, oh. A quarrel. Get used to them, boy. This is just the first of a million."

Not for me, it isn't, Owen thought. A man was a fool to put up with a woman's inconsistencies. He didn't have to, and he wasn't going to.

He said, "Good night, Tom," and stalked toward his horse. The reins scraped across those warts again. He was going to burn them off the first minute he got home.

He walked into the kitchen and rummaged around in the cupboard until he found the bottle of nitric acid. He held his finger over the wash pan and poured a drop of acid on each of the warts. It stung like fire.

Molly walked into the kitchen and asked, "What are you doing?"

"Burning warts off my finger."

Her face was concerned. "Isn't that dangerous?"

"I've done it before," he said grumpily.

He dipped water from the bucket and poured it over his finger. The stinging fire wouldn't stop.

Molly said, "I hope it doesn't bother you Saturday."

"I'm not going to the celebration." He wouldn't look at her.

She said quietly, "I thought you returned pretty quick. What did you and Evlalie fight about?"

"Not much," he said gloomily. "She's going with Clell Sawtelle."

Molly frowned. "That's not like Evlalie. I can't believe she would make a choice between you."

Owen said, honestly, "I didn't get around to asking her until tonight." He washed the finger again. The stinging wouldn't stop. He must have burned those warts to the roots. Anger showed in his eyes. "It looks to me like she was afraid no one would ask her. She grabbed the first one who did."

Molly said, "I never saw a smart man where a woman was concerned. You're mad at her because she didn't wait for you to ask her. And you wait until the last minute before you do."

He protested, "When did I have the time? She knows how busy I've been. No, she wanted to go with Sawtelle."

"She wanted to wake you up. You've been taking her for granted for quite a while now. A woman can't take that. She has to be a part of a man's life. I'll bet when you ride over there you spend a lot of time talking to Tom Denton."

He said defensively, "He wants to know how things are over here."

"And you tell him. Then you want to know how things are over there. And Evlalie wonders whether you came over to see her or her father. Didn't you ever watch Clell Sawtelle around a woman? Nobody else exists but her. He makes her feel important."

Owen's face was stiff. "If that's what Evlalie wants—"

"It's what you've forced her to. You were planning on punishing her by not going to the celebration."

Owen squirmed. It sounded bad put into words.

"She might have a good time," Molly reminded him. "You're gambling. She might have a better time with Clell."

"Let her." His outrage didn't ring true. Suppose Molly was right. It scared him.

Molly said, "You go to that celebration and tell her you're sorry. Show her you're sorry. That will reach her quicker than anything. A little misunderstanding doesn't seem important at first. But unless that little crack is mended, it will spread until you can't shout across it."

Owen hugged her. He would look so miserable that Evlalie couldn't help but be touched. He said, "Are all women as wise as you?"

Molly's eyes were troubled. "Not all of them. You take care of that finger."

He washed the finger again after she left. He couldn't get the fire out of it. Maybe he should have diluted that acid.

The hand was swollen the morning of the celebration. It hadn't let Owen sleep much the past two nights. The ache kept honing a sharp edge to his disposition.

It wasn't going to be a happy day if he stayed with the family. Enoch was in a sulky mood, not wanting to return to town so soon after his licking. Owen heard him tell Molly, "I'll split the head of the first nester, who laughs at me."

Molly said wearily, "You'll do nothing of the kind. Can't we have one enjoyable day?"

Enoch looked at Letty, and the dislike in his eyes was a wicked flame. What happened didn't help her standing with Enoch, Owen thought. She's Linus's daughter.

Chad was sullen. He didn't speak a word during breakfast. Owen knew the symptoms. Chad and Letty had quarreled. People seemed to do that better than anything else.

Letty babbled with excitement about the coming day. She had a new green silk dress, cut extremely low at the neckline. Molly looked at that neckline, then at Chad, and there was worry in her eyes.

Letty talked all the way into town. Enoch drove the buggy, and Owen rode behind him. He could see the red in Enoch's neck, and he expected that at any moment, Enoch would tell her to shut up.

The family split when they reached town. Chad and Letty wandered off together. Enoch headed for a group of old friends. He could tell his story of mistreatment to fresh, sympathetic ears. Molly found other ranchers' wives.

Owen was left alone. He looked all over town and couldn't find Evlalie or Sawtelle. It was hot, and traffic up and down the main street kept dust hanging in the air. The hand kept aching. The swelling was half way up his forearm. It honed away at that sharp edge to his disposition.

He was sorry they had arrived in town so early. There wasn't much to do. The main street looked festive with bunting and flags, but already the decorations were getting a dusty, wilted look. He watched a bunch of kids shoot some firecrackers. He looked at their happy, excited faces. Kids were lucky. They filled their lives with simple things.

A half-dozen cowboys galloped down the street, banging their pistols at the sky. Kilmonte must have relaxed his restrictions for the day. The dust the horses raised settled about

Owen. It stuck to his sweating skin, leaving him feeling itchy.

He made another tour of the town. Evlalie and Sawtelle still weren't here. He kept picking at the question of what they were doing, and the lack of an answer was a burr under his saddle.

In the afternoon, he listened to three speeches by local politicians. Politicians sounded all alike. They spoke the same words, such as this great and glorious country, and they used the same ringing tones. The trick was not to listen to their words, but then those ringing tones put a man to sleep.

He passed Kilmonte on the street, and they nodded to each other. The lack of liking was in those cool nods. He didn't envy Kilmonte his job today. The town was filled with different factions and keeping them apart would take constant alertness. Particularly, when those factions got to drinking.

He stopped at Hillsdale's saloon, more out of sheer boredom than the need for a drink. He ordered a beer, and it tasted flat and tepid. The place was filled, and he listened to talk and laughter. He wasn't a part of any of it. A man could sure get himself cut off from the world.

Hillsdale served sandwiches, and Owen ordered one. The meat in it was tasteless. He might just as well be chewing on a piece of flannel. He didn't want any more of that tepid beer, either. He ordered a shot of whiskey and followed it with another. He could feel the two shots kicking around in his belly like an angry mule. The liquor made him hotter, but he didn't care.

He went out to look for Evlalie and Sawtelle again. He made three more rounds of the town and in between each of them he had a shot of whiskey. It gave him something to do.

He found them at sundown. They were picnicking in the shade of a tree on the outskirts of town. He said, "Evlalie," and her eyes were distant as she looked at him.

Sawtelle was in high good spirits. He said, "We knew the town would be hot. We didn't come in until now. I say, old chap, you don't look fresh."

Owen knew how he looked. His clothing was rumpled and sticking to his skin. His boots were dust-covered. He said, "Evlalie, I want to talk to you." He had trouble with her name and had to repeat it.

"Not now." Her hands were busy laying out the food.

He saw the fried chicken and the hard-boiled eggs. She set a big, three-layered, white cake on the cloth, and he remembered the tasteless sandwich. The whiskey punched at the emptiness in his stomach, and the whiskey won. The edge on his disposition was pretty sharp now.

"When?" he demanded.

She gave him a cool appraisal. Some acid rejoinder trembled on her tongue, but Sawtelle was watching them, and she held it. She said, "At the dance."

He could press this and force a quarrel. The whiskey push wasn't that strong.

He said, "Thanks, Ev," and the belligerence was gone from his tone. He saw some flick of emotion he could not read in her eyes.

He turned away and thought, Molly might as well have talked to a tree. He hadn't paid any attention to what she told him. What made a man so pigheaded? Jealousy? He admitted it was the answer. He was jealous of the attention Evlalie was paying Sawtelle. She went to a lot of trouble preparing that picnic.

He wanted to look back, and he held his head stiffly forward. It would be different tonight. He would show her how sorry he was. Dismay flooded him as he thought, what if she doesn't care how sorry you are? That couldn't happen. He wouldn't let it happen.

He was at the dance early, and Evlalie wasn't there. Dancing was going to be hot work tonight. He saw several men slip out of the schoolhouse to the jugs they had hidden outside. That liquor wasn't going to cool them off. The whiskey push was gone in him. He had stopped and cleaned up at the livery stable. Hoyt's facilities were poor, but at least, Owen had washed his face and shined his boots with a rub rag. The hand and arm hurt. The swelling was up to his elbow. He tried to close his mind to it.

Enoch and Molly came in, and Molly looked flushed and tired. She said, "Isn't it funny how you can look forward to something, when you know the doing of it will wear you out?"

Owen grinned. Next year she would look forward to the celebration just as eagerly.

He asked, "Have you seen Chad and Letty?"

"They were right behind us," Enoch growled. "Chad's packing a load."

Owen thought, oh, no. Chad didn't often drink, but he could be a wild man, when he did. It sounded as if Chad's quarrel with Letty still existed, and he was trying to drown it in liquor.

Molly said, "Calm him down, Owen."

He nodded. He would try. But about the only thing that could calm Chad was Letty. He thought gloomily, a woman always held a big club.

Chad and Letty came in a few minutes later. The liquor shine was in his eyes, and his walk wasn't quite steady. His mouth always had that tight, pinched look when he was mad. It had it now.

Letty glowed with some kind of an inner excitement, and Owen thought, she enjoys baiting him.

Letty tickled Owen under the chin and giggled. A shine was in those black eyes as she asked, "You'll dance with me, won't you, Owen?"

Owen saw the dark flicker in Chad's eyes. He said, "Ask me later." If Letty pulled that little, intimate gesture with some other man, Chad would explode.

He sighed and remained at the door. Evlalie and Sawtelle came in after the music started.

Owen asked, "Ev, will you save a dance for me?"

Refusal was in her eyes, when Sawtelle said, "Certainly she will, old man."

He didn't see the flash of anger in Evlalie's eyes. A woman made her own decision in matters like this. Perhaps Sawtelle didn't know as much about women as Molly said he did.

Owen said gravely, "I'll come over to claim it."

He stood against the wall, watching the dancers. Sawtelle was graceful, and Evlalie floated like a leaf. She kept laughing up into Sawtelle's face at things he said. Owen was going to have to keep his head. Sawtelle was a lot of competition.

Letty came over and pulled at Owen's arm. "Dance with me."

Chad stood in a corner, watching sullenly.

Owen shook his head. "It's the first dance. Go dance with your husband."

She shook her head impatiently. "He can't dance. And he's too drunk to stand up." An impotent anger was in her eyes. No matter how she tried, she couldn't make this man notice her. If he once held her in his arms, he would be aware of her. She knew that.

Owen said, "Letty, help him. He's hurting pretty bad."

Letty gave him a hostile glance as she moved away. She passed two men and gave them a smile. It was an alluring smile, as beckoning as a crooking finger. Chad saw it, for he turned and plunged out of the room. Owen supposed he was after another belt of whiskey. Enoch saw it, too. Owen saw the harsh, frozen set of his face. Letty was stirring up trouble, and she didn't have to work hard at it at all.

When Chad came back in, Letty was dancing with Alderson. Alderson owned the general store. He was a fat fool with a fixed, fatuous grin on his face. He must have had a few drinks to fail to recognize the black look on Chad's face.

Owen felt the building tension. It throbbed in unison with the ache in his arm. It was a bad day, and he would be glad when it was over.

It was the fifth dance before he could claim Evlalie. Letty hadn't missed a dance, and none of them were with Chad. Other men, emboldened by Alderson's success, were giving her a rush. She loved it; she was having the time of her life.

It was hard to watch her and Chad and keep his attention on Evlalie. He said, "I'm sorry, Ev."

"For what?" The indifference was still in her voice.

Oh, hell! He managed to keep from putting it into words. He wanted to talk to her; he needed her sympathy. He turned her so that he could watch Letty. Dougan was dancing with her, and he held her pretty tight. He was a fool. Couldn't he see the glitter in Chad's eyes.

Owen said, "For not being with you today. I've missed you." She nodded. He thought there was a softening in her.

He leard Letty's giggle and twisted his head. Dougan had said something that struck a response from her. Chad moved, and Owen was ready to intercept him, if he went after Dougan. But Chad turned and staggered outdoors. Another drink or two, and Chad would fight, or fall on his face.

Owen looked at Evlalie and asked, "What makes a woman be such a damned fool?"

He wasn't really conscious of putting the thought into words. And he certainly didn't have any intention that it applied to her.

He felt her body stiffen in his arms. He was tired and troubled over Chad. A fight was the last thing the Parnells wanted here this evening. And one was brewing unless Chad quit drinking, or unless Letty got some sense into her head.

"Ah, Ev," he said. "Stop it. You're always jumping to conclusions. You know how I feel about you."

"Do I? You should tell me sometime."

Her mouth was tight. He must be saying everything wrong. He tried to watch the door and Letty at the same time.

Evlalie said, "If you're that interested in her, why don't you dance with her?"

Her inference left Owen speechless for a moment. He found his tongue and said, "If you haven't got enough sense to know better—" He tried to bite it off. It was too late.

Her eyes were furious. "I didn't want to talk to you. I didn't want to dance with you." She pulled out of his arms and whirled. He was glad the music stopped then, or her action would have pulled every eye in the room to them.

He followed her back to Sawtelle. Sawtelle's face was anxious as he looked at them. It didn't take a keen observer to see dissension between them.

Owen's face was gloomy. Things were worse. Somehow, she had gotten the fool notion in her head that he was interested in Letty.

He said, "I'll see you later." The curt bob of her head wasn't agreement. It was dismissal.

The music started again, and he saw Dougan heading toward Letty. He angled across the floor to cut him off. He didn't want Chad coming back in and seeing Letty dancing again with Dougan.

He lifted his arms and said, "Dance?"

He saw the glow come into her eyes, and it made him uncomfortable. He looked down at her, and that low-cut neckline let him see too much of her ripe, full breasts. He knew a quick surge of anger at her and at Chad.

She came into his arms. He could feel the pressure of those firm breasts against his chest, and the room was suddenly too hot. He smelled the perfume she wore, and another, more basic smell was beneath it—the raw, beckoning smell of woman.

He said, "Letty, why don't you stop."

Triumph danced in her eyes. "Stop what?" she murmured.

Oh, Lord, Owen thought. She thinks I'm interested in her.

"Stop making Chad so miserable."

She shrugged, and the gesture said, who cares what happens to Chad?

He was wasting his time trying to appeal to her. She didn't know it, but she was leaving after this dance.

He passed Evlalie, and her face was cool and impersonal. Owen had left her and gone straight to Letty.

He thought the dance would never end. When it was over, he seized her wrist and led her to Enoch and Molly. "Keep her here," he said. "I'm going to corral Chad."

Enoch's eyes were filled with contempt as he looked at Letty. "We'll follow you out," he said.

Owen hated that distressed look in Molly's eyes. She was trying to keep her head high and proud, but this was hurting. Tomorrow, he was going to talk straight and hard to Letty.

He hurried outdoors and heard loud voices from around the corner of the building. Chad said, "You keep your hands off me."

Owen ran around the corner. Chad leaned against the building, and Kilmonte stood in front of him.

Kilmonte's face was relieved at the sight of Owen. He said, "Ease him down, Owen. Or I'll have to arrest him. In a couple of minutes, he's going to try to tear up this building."

So Kilmonte had seen it coming, too. Owen knew a bitter shame. Everyone must be aware of it.

He said, "Come on, Chad. We're going home."

He tried to take Chad's arm, and Chad jerked it away. Chad's face went suddenly wild. "You're the sonuvabitch who's after my wife."

He lunged at Owen, not recognizing him. His hands were wide and clawing. He was too drunk to fight, but he was going to try.

Owen hit that wide-open chin. He hit it squarely, not saving the power. This would be the quickest and easiest way for Chad.

Chad's head flew back under the impact. His eyes rolled up into his head. He gave a tired, little sigh as he bent forward, then pitched onto his face.

Kilmonte tried to ease Owen's bitter expression. "It was the best way. He won't remember a thing."

"You keep your damned mouth shut," Owen said passionately.

Kilmonte said, "By God, Owen. I'm getting tired of the name Parnell."

Before he could say more, Enoch and Molly came around the corner. Enoch had Letty by the arm and was jerking her along with him.

He saw Chad's unconscious form, and temper flared in his face. He asked Owen, "What did Kilmonte hit him for?"

Kilmonte's face was raw and violent. Owen said hastily, "I hit him." He heard Molly's distressed cry. "I couldn't do anything else. He didn't know who I was. He was determined to jump someone."

Molly sat down beside Chad and took his head in her lap. "He isn't hurt, is he?"

"No, ma'am," Kilmonte said. "He might have a headache in the morning. No more."

Enoch said stiffly, "We can take care of our own."

Kilmonte's patience was rubbed too thin. "Take him and get out of town. Right now." He locked eyes with Enoch. He said against the truculence in Enoch's face, "If you don't think I mean it, try me."

They had pushed Kilmonte pretty far. Owen said quietly, "We're going, John. Just as soon as I can bring the buggy around."

He drove the buggy back, and he and Enoch loaded Chad's limp weight into the back seat. Chad stirred a little and muttered.

"Get in beside him, Letty," Owen ordered. "And help prop him up."

Letty's face filled with rebellion. "It's early. I don't want to go home."

Enoch whirled on her. "You shut up," he said savagely. "You hear me. Just shut up."

Owen climbed in on the other side of Chad. Chad's head lolled from his shoulder to Letty's. Enoch and Molly took the front seat. It was a strained trip. Now and then, Chad muttered a word, breaking the silence. Once, in a clear voice he said, "Letty."

Just as they came in sight of the house Enoch said, "I was sending Chad up tomorrow with supplies for Hamp and Scotty. But he won't be worth a damn. You'll have to take them. I want to know how things are."

Owen nodded wearily. He had planned on riding over to see Evlalie tomorrow. But maybe it would be just as well to let a day or two pass.

The darkness hid the shine in Letty's eyes. For a few minutes, Owen had held her close. She shivered as she remembered the hard feel of his chest against her breasts. He had been aware of her for those few moments. She knew it. But the family had been near, and he could do nothing about it. But tomorrow morning was a different time. She knew the route he would take. She knew the pool, formed by the spring in the foothills. If Owen surprised her, while she was taking her bath— Her pulses hammered. He would notice her then. He couldn't help but notice her.

TEN

The ache in Owen's arm kept him from sleeping much. The swelling was worse in the morning. It reached above his elbow, and he could feel its throbbing in his shoulder.

It was awkward dressing with one hand. He thought sourly of the trip ahead of him. He wished someone else were taking that ride.

He walked into the kitchen and searched through the cabinets for something to ease the pain. He never realized how awkward it was being a one-handed man. He knocked over a glass and a jar and swore. If he kept on, he would have everyone in the house awake.

Molly came into the kitchen, stifling a yawn. She said crossly, "Are you this eager to get started." She saw his contrite face, and her crossness disappeared. "You didn't wake me. I didn't sleep well."

She wouldn't. She would lie awake, worrying about Chad and Letty, trying to get some sort of workable hold on their problem.

She looked at Owen's swollen hand. Her face was immediately concerned. "I told you that was a dangerous thing to do," she said. "Now you've caught cold in it."

THE LONG COLD WIND

Owen grimaced. He wouldn't argue with her.

She rummaged in the back of a cupboard and found a large, brown bottle. The label said it was Merchants Gargling Oil, a liniment good for man and beast. "Take off your shirt," she ordered. She poured some of the liquid into a pan and soaked a piece of cloth in it. She wrapped Owen's arm and hand in several folds of the cloth. The liniment had a sting of its own.

"You'll do no riding today," she said.

He shook his head. "Hamp and Scotty need those supplies."

Her voice was tart. "What's wrong with Enoch taking them?"

Enoch came into the kitchen and grunted as he saw them. The grunt could have been the morning's greeting, or approval of their early arising.

Before Enoch could speak, Molly jumped him. "Look at his arm," she said. She made it sound as though the swollen arm was Enoch's fault, and she put him on the defensive. "Do you think he can ride with it? He's going to stay here and let me doctor it."

"All right, all right," Enoch grumbled. "I'll wake up Chad."

"You will not. He'll be in no shape to do anything today. Besides, I want to talk to him and Letty."

Enoch glared at her. "Then I'll get Les or Abel."

"You told them they could stay in town last night," she pointed out.

Owen hid his grin. She was hemming Enoch in, forcing him to face an obvious choice.

"Do I have to do everything around here?" he roared.

"You will today," she said firmly.

He stalked out of the kitchen, slamming the door behind him.

Molly looked at Owen and shook her head. "He's so mad he won't eat any breakfast." She poured more liniment on the cloth. Her face was anxious. "Does it feel any better?"

He thought it did. Or maybe the sting of the liniment was stronger than the ache.

Letty left the house at daybreak. Her eyes were wide and excited, and a hammering was in her breast. Most of the night she had lain awake beside Chad, listening to his heavy snoring. The sour odor of his whiskey-laden breath was in the room, and she thought fiercely, I don't want him touching me again.

But Owen— Ah, that was a different matter. Each time she thought of him, a delicious tingling wave washed over her. She was shameless and brazen. She admitted it and did not care. But she could belong to a man like Owen. She would belong to him after this morning. When he saw her, standing in that pool, he would be unable to resist her. What would happen after this morning she did not know or care. From then on, it would be Owen's problem.

She saddled and turned toward the foothills. She looked back at the house, and her eyes were furtive as if she expected someone to stop her. But no one would miss her. Chad would sleep most of the morning, and the others would think she was with him. She wondered how far ahead of Owen she would be. It didn't matter. She could wait with all the outward patience in the world. But inwardly, there would be no patience at all.

The morning air had chill in it. With the rising of the sun, the chill would quickly dissipate. The trail made a bend just before it reached the pool. She would hear the rider before she saw him. She would turn as he came into view, squealing in surprise and embarrassment. He would sit there and look at her, and she would see the hot blood rushing into his face. She kicked her pony into a faster pace.

Enoch swore as he rode. The way Molly babied those boys was a crime. Because Owen had a little swelling in his arm and Chad wasn't feeling good—He shook his head in disgust and jerked on the unwilling pack animal's lead. Damn it. He had other things he wanted to do today.

The spring-fed pool was just around the bend. He would stop there and let the animals water. He mopped his sleeve across his forehead. The sun was already like a club. It would be hotter on the ride back.

He came out of the turn, and his jaw dropped. He blinked his eyes several times. He must still be asleep. He couldn't be seeing what he saw. A naked woman was in the pool, standing in water to her knees. Her long, black hair streamed down her back. She turned slowly to face him.

He saw the full, ripe breasts, the rounded belly. He saw the laughter on Letty's face fade to dismay.

His fury thickened his tongue until it had no room to move in his mouth. He remembered how she looked at Owen last night, he remembered how she pressed against him. Enoch never considered that Owen might return the interest. No, this was all Letty's doing. She had been in the buggy, when he told Owen to take the supplies to the summer camp. She had waited in this pool to trap him. It might have worked, he thought grimly. A young man's blood rose quickly, and that kind of heat blotted out clear thinking.

He sat there staring at her with those terrible eyes, until the shame rose hot in her face, and she tried to cover herself with her arms.

"You squaw," he said thickly. That was all she was, a squaw, who would bed with any man who looked at her.

Her eyes blazed at the contempt in the word, and she threw up her head and looked at him. They were bitter antagonists, but the strength was all on his side.

He said, "Get your clothes on," and turned his head, while she dressed.

He swung down and seized her arm, and the wince in her face told how cruelly his fingers bit. "You'll leave my house now," he said, the bitter triumph in his eyes. "You hear me?" His fingers bit deeper, and she was barely able to stifle an outcry. "You'll tell Chad you're through with him, and you'll be gone, when I get back. Or I'll tell him you were throwing yourself at his brother. I think he'd kill you for that."

She met his eyes, then her head fell. She was beaten. He could tell by the droop in her shoulders.

He mounted and rode off without looking back. He was rid of her. His eyes lit with a frosty glitter that was almost laughter.

Molly stormed at Enoch, when he rode into the yard. She hardly gave him time to light before her words poured at him.

He was hot and tired, and he said testily, "Here now. You're gabbling like a goose. Slow down."

She was white-faced with fury, and her rapid breathing kept tearing her words into shreds. Owen stood behind her, and his face had a black, accusing look.

Molly bit her lip, and her words slowed. "Chad's gone. He's gone with her."

"Gone," Enoch echoed stupidly.

She nodded. "He said, if he stayed here he'd kill you."

Enoch seized her shoulders. Something was wrong, tragically wrong. "What did she tell him?"

"That you came up on her, while she was bathing. That you made awful remarks to her. She was afraid you were coming in after her."

Enoch groaned inwardly though not a quiver of it showed in

his face. He had made a bad mistake. He had let her come back here first, when he should have brought her. But he had been trying to save Chad. He thought she would be frightened and ashamed enough to slink away. She was more clever and bold than he believed possible. She had told her twisted story first, and Chad believed her. Not only Chad. Molly and Owen.

He said quietly, "Molly. Do you believe her?"

She gave him a long, searching look, then she whimpered, "I guess it was Chad's leaving that shook me so." She pressed her face against his chest. "Oh, Enoch."

The black look left Owen's face. Molly believed him. That should be good enough for Owen. He asked, "What did happen?"

Enoch threw him a bleak look. "It was you she was waiting for. In that spring pool. She heard me tell you last night to take supplies up to the camp. She knew the trail you'd take. Would she ride that far to take a bath, when McDonald's creek is closer?"

Owen's face flamed as the implication sank in. "Do you think I had a hand in arranging—"

"No one's accusing you," Enoch said gruffly. "It was all in her mind. I'm glad she's gone. If Chad's damn fool enough to follow her, he'll learn about her soon enough."

"I'll go after him," Owen said. "When he hears the truth—"

"No," Enoch said heavily. "Do you think he'd believe you? He's got something to learn. He'll get no help from us in learning it."

The protest died on Owen's tongue. Enoch was right. Chad wouldn't believe him. He turned and followed Enoch and Molly toward the house. Enoch's arm was about Molly's shoulder. She was crying. She made no sound, but Owen could see her shoulders shaking under Enoch's arm.

ELEVEN

The heat ran through July and extended into August. The dry winds stripped the tired covering from the parched earth and tossed great clouds of dust into the air. A man lived with the taste and smell of dust. It was in his food, and even after a dipperful of water, he felt the grit in his teeth. The grit became sandpaper rasping human dispositions raw. Now a person became too keenly aware of the monotony of living, for today was like yesterday, and tomorrow would only bring more of the same.

Molly ran her finger across a table top, and complaint was in her voice. "You wouldn't think I'd dusted less than two hours ago."

Owen nodded absently. He was watching the road for Enoch's return. Maybe he should have ridden into town with him. At least it would have broken the monotony. But for the past month he had stayed stubbornly away from town, for fear he would bump into Evlalie. He did not want to see her again. He did not want an exchange of polite, cold words, words that meant nothing. She picked it this way, he thought, and the familiar rush of anger did not come. Instead, there was only a dismal sense of loss. But he couldn't do any more. He had ridden over to see her, shortly after Chad and Letty left. He was sure he caught a glimpse of Evlalie at the kitchen window, but Tom Denton had said she wasn't home. Denton's words had been evasive and lame, and Owen had said abruptly, "All right, Tom." He did not return. When a woman did not want to see a man, there was no way of breaking down the barrier.

Molly looked listless and tired, and there were circles under her eyes. Owen knew that heat wasn't draining her. She had gone through hot summers before. It was worry, worry over Chad.

Molly said, "He's been gone over six weeks. You'd think he'd come back at least once."

Owen placed his arm about her shoulders. "He'll come." There was no real assurance in his voice. Pride would keep Chad from returning, even to see Molly. He had made his stand, and he would not back down from it. Owen recalled some of the wild, savage words the day Chad left with Letty. Chad didn't need anything Enoch Parnell had. He would starve before he would take anything from Enoch. Owen hoped Chad never had to eat any of those words.

He thought, he will not be back until he is rid of Letty. That might take years. A man's need of a woman was a bit in his mouth, and he was helpless to go in the direction he pleased, until the bit was removed.

He looked out the window and saw the buckboard. "Enoch's coming," he said.

"I hope he didn't forget my thread," Molly said.

Owen helped carry the supplies into the house. Enoch had a grim set to his face. He had run into something in town that displeased him. He would talk about it, when the time suited him. Or he would not talk at all. Ever since Chad left, this house was filled with too much silence. Enoch would stare at nothing, and no one knew what he was thinking. You could tell what Molly was thinking. The longing was plain in her eyes.

At supper, Enoch pushed back his plate and said, "I'm not hungry."

Molly's temper was near the surface. "What's wrong with it?" she demanded.

Enoch gave her a heavy glance. "I didn't say anything was wrong with it." He sat and stared at the far wall.

He said suddenly, "I ran into McLaughlin in town."

Owen laid down his knife and fork. He saw Molly's face light up. They knew Chad had gone to work for McLaughlin. It didn't seem possible, but Enoch might relay some news about Chad.

"Did he say anything about—" Molly faltered under Enoch's probing eyes.

"He said enough." That was angry color rising from Enoch's collar. "McLaughlin apologized to me. Chad didn't last a month with him. McLaughlin had to pay him off and let him go."

Molly cried, "Why?"

This was galling to Enoch's pride, his own son not being able to hold a job. He said heatedly, "He traded on my name to get the job, and then he couldn't hold it."

Molly was tight-lipped at Enoch's unfairness. Chad was a capable hand. He could ask for a job on his own merits. "Why did McLaughlin let him go?"

Enoch exploded. "That damned woman. He's so filled with her he can't keep his mind on a job. McLaughlin didn't have anyplace for her. Chad kept riding into town to see her."

Molly said indignantly, "That's only natural. McLaughlin might have understood."

Owen thought, no, Molly. None of us understood. You couldn't expect McLaughlin to. If we'd tried a little harder, Chad might still be here.

Enoch stood and banged his fist on the table. "I don't want to hear any more about it."

Molly met his anger with equal defiance. "I want to talk about it. Was Chad in town?"

"How do I know? I didn't look for him." There was an evasive flicker in his eyes. Enoch had seen or heard of Chad.

Molly drew a deep breath. "Enoch Parnell, if you're lying to me—"

Enoch glared at her and left the room. If Molly kept pressing him, she'd have him tripping over his tongue.

Owen tried to ease Molly's anger. "Chad's in town. If Letty's there, you know Chad's there. I doubt if Enoch saw or talked to him. He just probably heard Chad was there."

He knew what was coming before Molly could ask him. His voice was gruff. "I was thinking of riding into town tonight, anyway." He admitted he wanted to see Chad.

"He'll need money, Owen. I've patched those old shirts of his. He didn't take half his stuff. His old boots and hat—" Her brow furrowed in concentration as she ticked off the items.

Owen groaned in mock despair. She would load him like a

pack horse. He said, "We're not even sure he's there. I'll find out. He can pick up those things, himself."

"But if he needs them "

"If he needs them, he'll be after them," Owen said gently.

Molly stood and moved to a cupboard.

Owen knew she was after the sugar jar, in which she kept money. He said, "I've got money."

She turned, and her face worked with emotion. "Owen, tell him " She stopped and bit her lip.

He nodded gravely. She didn't have to say it. Tell Chad she missed him, that she was worried about him.

He brushed her forehead with his lips as he passed her. "I'll get back as soon as I can." Enoch was going to raise hell, when he heard about this trip.

Letty sat before the chipped, distorted mirror, brushing her hair. Cully stood behind her, staring at her. Liquor glistened in the shine of his eyes, in the beads of sweat that popped out on his forehead. He tried to hold himself rigidly erect, but she could see the small sway to his shoulders.

She had an audience, and she was enjoying herself. "It was awful, Cully. You just don't know how bad it was. Now I have to live like this." She half turned and waved the hair brush at the poor, little room. She really didn't mind the rented room with its meager furniture. It was better than living at the Parnell's. At least, she didn't have Enoch's cold eyes following her every move; she didn't have Molly sighing with resignation as she picked up after her.

No, she didn't mind this room at all, while Chad was working for McLaughlin. The trouble was that the job hadn't lasted long enough. She hadn't minded the first week Chad was back in town. He had gambled that first week and won. It wasn't hard to laugh with him, when he came into the room and emptied his pockets on the bed. He pulled money from every pocket, and she remembered the tight, triumphant feeling in her throat as she looked at it. She didn't need the Parnells. Chad could take care of her. He had showered gifts on her. Behind the sheet across the corner of the room were four new dresses. That week was the way to live. It had been easy for her to laugh with Chad, it had been easy to be kind to him. Since that week, he had been losing. Even though he wouldn't talk about it, she could tell by the strain in his face. At times, fear of the future knotted in her stomach before she could toss it aside. She could get along, with or without him. If a husband couldn't support his wife, she didn't have to stay with him.

She gave Cully a brave, little smile. "I don't mind this room too much."

Cully couldn't see what she was talking about. The room looked all right to him. He asked, "What did he do to you?" He had trouble saying a couple of the words.

She remembered Enoch Parnell's dirty, old eyes going over her as she stood in the pool. She would never forget the shame of that moment. She had convinced herself that Owen was responsible, that if he had taken the supplies as he was supposed to have, none of this would have happened.

She made a vague gesture. "Nothing really, I guess. But he would say awful things to me. And he was always trying to get me to go into the barn or someplace with him. He spied on me all the time. I couldn't even go to the outhouse, without " She blushed and did not finish.

"That Goddamned Owen," Cully said savagely. He knew how Letty had been treated. Her Indian blood made her easy prey for any white man, who looked at her. She had been all alone at the Parnells. She couldn't tell Chad what was happening, for he would side with his brother and wouldn't believe her. He did give a grudging bit of credit to Chad. When Owen forced Letty to leave, Chad had gone with her.

He took a step and lurched. He threw his hand to the back of the chair for support. He said wildly, "I'll kill him, when I see him."

The words didn't alarm Letty. They were whiskey words, forgotten when Cully awakened in the morning. She said, "Don't think about it, Cully. I'm trying to forget it."

She watched his unsteady course toward the door. After a few more drinks, Cully would fall asleep. She looked at the mirror and resumed brushing her hair, humming a little tune. She hoped Chad stayed out the entire night.

It wasn't hard for Owen to learn Chad and Letty were living in town. Chad's horse was at the livery stable, and Alderson, in the general store, said, "I'm not going to give him any more credit. When a man tries to live by gambling—" He shook his head self-righteously.

You bastard, Owen thought. You would have gone after his

wife quickly enough. "I'll pay his bill," he snapped. He stared at Alderson until the man colored. "You let him have what he needs."

Alderson laughed nervously. "Why sure, Owen. Just as long as I know he's got something in back of him."

Owen raged inwardly as he left the store. Alderson was a pillar of the town. He ran his business honestly, and he was a deacon in the church. He was a damned hypocrite, but the town couldn't see it.

Owen saw Kilmonte at the end of the block and would have turned in another direction, but it was too late. Kilmonte was moving toward him.

He said, "Owen," and Owen nodded. Kilmonte rolled a cigarette and said, "This damned heat. Will it ever break?"

Owen waited. Kilmonte had something else on his mind besides the heat.

Kilmonte asked casually, "You looking for Chad?"

"I might be."

"He's in Hillsdale's saloon." Kilmonte had something else to say, and he fumbled with it.

Owen gave him no help.

"Is he going back with you?"

Owen said challengingly, "You tell me where that fits in with your job."

He heard the rush of Kilmonte's breathing. Kilmonte was no friend of theirs. He would prod him every time he could.

Kilmonte shook his head. "I don't know why I bother. Except that I'm trying to save everybody trouble. Chad's got that woman in his blood. He's gambling and losing. If he needs money bad enough, he could turn pretty wild."

"What are you accusing him of, John?"

"Nothing now. But it could happen." He looked at that wooden face, and a quick resentment filled his eyes. "If I have to go after him, you and Enoch will be the first to squawk. But you won't do a damned thing to head it off."

He moved past Owen, his shoulder almost brushing him. The hard thrust of his weight on his boot heels made the sidewalk ring.

Kilmonte had a right to his anger. But Owen couldn't tell him so. It was still family business. He was Chad's brother, but he was just as helpless as Kilmonte felt. All he could do was to look on and wait.

He felt heavy and depressed as he moved on down the street.

The poker game was in progress at one of the back tables in Hillsdale's saloon. Six men were seated at the table, and four others watched. Chad looked up and saw Owen approaching, and a quick flash of greeting was in his eyes. It was immediately veiled, and his face looked hard and impassive.

Owen nodded to him and waited. He knew better than to try to call Chad out of this game. By the size of the stack of chips before Chad, Owen would not have to wait long. Chad was in a losing streak. His nervous fingers kept stacking and restacking the few chips, and his eyes had a feverish shine. He was in with a bunch of wolves. Hillery and Bateman and Stivers were accomplished poker players, and Eldering was only a cut below them. Against their skill, Chad had only inexperience. It would take a tremendous run of luck to make Chad even with them.

A half-dozen pots cleaned Chad. He tried to force his cards, and he didn't have enough money to protect himself. He threw down his cards, swept the table with a quick, savage look, and pushed to his feet. He paused a moment, his face working with some indecisiveness, then he turned from the table.

Owen hid his relief as he fell into step with him. He had been tense there, fearing which direction Chad would break. He said, "I'll buy a drink."

Chad shook his head and continued on out of the building. Outside, he gained some semblance of control. His grin didn't quite come off as he said, "They cleaned me."

"It happens," Owen said gravely.

"My luck was changing." A wildness was in Chad, thrusting for expression. "I could feel it."

It was the cry of the loser. Owen's face didn't change. "Sure," he said.

Chad's face turned suspicious. "Did you come in to find me?"

Owen shook his head. He knew better than to say yes. He wished he could talk Chad into going back with him without Letty. "I came in for a drink. And to get away for a little while."

Chad nodded. "How's Molly?" His voice was gruff.

"Fine. The summer's pulling on her. She misses you."

Chad turned his head to keep Owen from seeing the quick working of emotion in his face. He said, "I'll see you around," and started to move away.

Owen caught his arm. "Chad, I've got thirty dollars—"

Chad's face flamed with passion. "I won't take his

Goddamned money. After what he did to Letty."

Owen shook his head. "My money, Chad. And I wasn't giving it to you. I thought a loan might let you find that lucky streak."

It was all he could do for Chad. Chad would probably fling this money after the money already lost. But Owen couldn't give it to him with a lecture on how to use it.

Chad's face broke for an instant, and his voice was rough. "I'd consider a loan."

Owen sensed the leap of hope in Chad as his hand closed on the money. The hope wouldn't last long, but at least, he had given him that much.

Chad said, "Thanks, Owen."

"Sure." Owen watched him re-enter Hillsdale's. He needed a drink, but not in Hillsdale's. Not where he could watch Chad. He moved toward Springman's feeling a heavy, depressing loneliness. The old days were gone and could never be brought back. The slight body of a woman stood between him and Chad. A granite mountain couldn't keep them farther apart.

Springman had one customer. The man's back was turned toward Owen, and Owen didn't recognize him. The customer was thoroughly drunk. He hung onto the bar for support and kept up a low, rumbling swearing. Springman turned worried eyes toward Owen, and Owen saw the relief flood them. Springman had an unruly one on his hands, and he was looking for help.

That was Kilmonte's job, Owen thought irritably. He wasn't getting involved with a drunk tonight. He picked the far end of the bar, putting as much distance between himself and the man as he could. He avoided looking at him. It took such a little thing to set a drunk off.

Springman came to him and said, "He keeps demanding another drink. He's had too much now." His voice was shaky, and sweat glistened on his bald head.

The man looked at Owen and shouted, "Are you talking about me?"

Strain tightened Owen's face. Cully's eyes were trouble hungry. Owen wished he hadn't picked Springman's. It might be best, if he turned and left. A stubbornness seized him. He would drink where he pleased, and Cully Derks wouldn't run him.

He said coldly, "No, Cully. We weren't." He took the bottle Springman shoved toward him and poured the shot.

Cully shuffled toward him, his eyes raw and quarrelsome. "I want a drink."

Owen shrugged. "It's not my bottle. I don't own the place."

Lightning shot through Cully's smoky eyes. "No," he shouted. "But you think you own everybody else."

Owen set down his empty glass.

Springman said, "Cully, that's enough. I won't have "

Owen waved him quiet. Anything Springman said would be a further irritant. "Cully. I didn't come in here looking for trouble."

He looked at the hating in those black eyes. He doubted Cully even heard him. Cully was beyond reason.

His hand closed on the neck of the bottle. It was half-filled, and he wished it were full. He intended no arguing with Cully. The quickest way of stopping this was the best.

Cully thrust his face toward Owen. "Pick on me," he shouted. He called Owen every vile name at his command. "No man would hound a woman like you did her."

It was difficult for Owen to keep a grip on his temper. He's probably referring to Letty, he thought bleakly. Letty was turning out to be quite an expert in turning a story to favor her.

He made one last effort. "You're drunk, Cully. Go home and sleep it off."

"Why, Goddamn you," Cully raged. "Don't be telling me what to do." The whiskey and his rage combined into one great force, pushing him forward.

He lunged at Owen, and Owen was ready for the move. He heard Springman's squawl as he sidestepped Cully's rush. He brought the bottle viciously down on Cully's head and felt the shock of the impact in his hand and arm as the bottle broke. The hat muffled some of the force, but still it should have been enough to drop him. It would have dropped a sober man. The liquor was holding up Cully.

Cully staggered back with wobbly steps, flinging his hands out for support. He blinked his eyes several times, and his face was dazed.

Owen held the jagged neck of the bottle, and he felt a vicious impulse to use it. He let it drop and moved at Cully before his eyes cleared. He slugged him with the left hand, then the right, both blows landing full in the face. Cully's head rocked back, pulling his body with it, but he stayed on his feet. He came back, his body soaking up punishment like a sponge. At the moment, he was a sponge, soaked in liquor, and the whiskey threw up a wall against the pain that would come later.

Owen looked at the bleeding mouth. "Cully, you can stop this right here."

The insane glitter in Cully's eyes was his answer. Cully had no skill with his fists, but his determination balanced some of the lack. He bored forward, his arms outstretched, hoping to get a hold of Owen. His dogged persistence was an awesome thing.

Owen kept moving before those clawing fingers. He hit the man at will, and Cully didn't even grunt. His face was a bloodied mess. His breathing formed and broke red bubbles at his nose and mouth. No one blow would drop him. It would take the cumulative effect of many blows.

Owen kept chipping away at this shuffling rock, draining away a bit of strength each time he hit him. Cully got close enough to fasten a hand on Owen's sleeve. Owen jerked his arm and heard material rip. The sleeve was left in Cully's fingers.

He panted as he waited for Cully. His face stung, and he guessed Cully's nails had scraped his cheek. He could feel the weariness pulling at his legs and arms. It didn't take much of this violent effort to make a man's muscles heavy.

Cully was in bad shape. The cumulative effect was showing. His face dripped blood, and he grunted each time he took a step. His head was sagging, and his arms moved as if great weights were attached to them.

But he was coming again, and the glitter remained in his eyes. Owen took a side step, and his foot came down on a cuspidor. It rolled under his weight, and his left knee came unhinged, throwing him up against the bar. Without its support, he would have gone down.

Cully grunted hoarsely and leaped forward. The bar hampered Owen's movements, penning him in. He chopped at Cully with short, vicious blows but he could not keep him away. From somewhere in his ebbing vitality, Cully found a tremendous, explosive burst of strength. Owen fought a crazy, wild animal, and he could not keep it off him. Cully kept him pinned against the bar, and his repeated lunges drove the edge of the bar into Owen's back. He butted with his head, he lifted and used his knees, and their impact sent rolling waves of shock through Owen's body. He clawed and butted and kicked, and the sound coming from his throat was an animal's snarl.

The contact lasted only a few seconds, but as brief as it was,

Owen took a terrible mauling. It left his senses reeling and pulled the strength from his muscles. For an instant, he thought Springman must have turned off the lamps, for a wall of blackness rolled and surged a few feet from him. He knew that if he went down, he wouldn't get up, for Cully would stamp him to pulp.

He rolled along the edge of the bar and managed to free an arm. He chopped his fist into Cully's throat, and the snarl changed to a gargled grunt. He slammed a knee into Cully's crotch, and the sickened puff of breath forced Cully's mouth open. Owen felt the sapping weakness creep through the man. He slashed at Cully's arms, and they bent under the impact, slipping from his body. He twisted and was free. His legs were wobbly, wanting to reject the hurried steps he demanded. He moved out from the bar a half-dozen steps and planted his feet wide to stay erect. His lungs were filled with fire, and his breathing was raspy. He kept shaking his head to clear the fog from his vision.

Only a remnant of his shirt was left. The rest was torn away by Cully's clawing hands. He looked with detached curiosity at the bruises and discolorations on his chest and stomach. It looked as if he had been underneath the angry hoofs of a herd of horses.

Cully clung to the bar for support. His knees insisted upon bending, and he would sag toward the floor, then pull himself back up. His face was turned toward Owen, but the glitter was gone from his eyes. They were dull and sick.

Owen stepped toward him. Cully tried to raise an arm to protect his face. Owen sledged him in the mouth again and again. Cully was defenseless as a tree to hit, and like a tree he seemed to be as firmly rooted. Owen knew a cold and merciless rage. None of this had been necessary, but Cully had pushed it. Maybe he wasn't the one responsible for it, but Owen couldn't hit Letty. So he pounded at Cully to alleviate that consuming rage.

He hit Cully and saw the tottering run through the man. He stepped back and let him fall. Even then, it took a little time. Cully half turned, his hands groping blindly before him. He tried to take a step, and his knee broke, pitching him forward on his face. He rolled over on his back, and Owen heard his harsh, labored breathing. Cully wasn't unconscious. His eyes were open and blank. He had no conscious thought in his head, but he

101

kept trying to push himself up. His arms buckled at the first thrust of weight against them.

Owen stared blankly at him. The rage was gone, leaving only a weakening weariness. He turned to the bar and said, "A drink." His jaws hurt, and that rasping voice sounded like a stranger's.

Springman's eyes were big with awe. "I didn't think you were going to do it. He's crazy, Owen."

Owen nodded, and there was agreement in the gesture to both of Springman's statements. He gulped the shot of whiskey, and the warm wave flowing from his stomach pushed strength into his body.

"I'll get Kilmonte," Springman said.

"No," Owen said. "It wasn't Cully's fault." He felt a sort of pity for Cully and certainly a respect. "No," he said again.

He rolled the empty glass in his fingers. Would a second shot help him, or make him feel more tired? He had no desire to see Cully thrown into jail. Cully had more than enough punishment for one night.

He saw Springman's face go tight. Springman was trying to say something, but it seemed as if some sudden apparition had frozen his tongue.

Owen heard the scratching sound behind him. He was turning, when Springman yelled, "Owen. Look out."

Owen finished his turn and saw Cully coming at him. Disbelief dulled his senses and made his reaction time slow. It wasn't possible, but Cully was on his feet. He held a chair in his hands, and his wrecked face worked convulsively. The wild glitter was back in his eyes.

He swung the chair. Owen picked out the motion. He watched it come toward him almost curiously. There wasn't time to step aside, or even to duck. He did manage to throw up an arm. The swinging chair knocked it aside, and Owen felt the quick slash of pain run the length of his arm. The chair bottom smashed into the side of his face with stunning impact. A million lights exploded before his eyes. Then somebody extinguished them all at once.

TWELVE

Owen regained consciousness in Doc Rockwood's office. He didn't want to open his eyes. If he did, he would admit pain. Great waves of it were just beyond his closed eyes. He lay there, trying to localize the pain. His face felt stiff, and there was a throbbing in his jaw. He couldn't tell exactly where the pain started. He only knew he had a lot of it.

He opened his eyes and wished he hadn't. The light from the lamp was blinding. He blinked against it and tried to speak. His jaw wouldn't move well, and his voice came out a stiff croak.

Doc Rockwood leaned forward and said, "How's it feel?" He was a small man with a sour face and a gruff manner. His eyes were as mournful as a hound dog's. No one knew Doc's personal history. No one dared ask him about it, for fear he'd snap off their heads. His hands did not fit his manner. His hands were gentle.

Owen stared at Kilmonte with puzzled eyes. What was he doing here? Springman was also in the room. Owen knew where he was. This was Doc Rockwood's office, but how did he get here?

Kilmonte said, "Cully broke your jaw."

Memory trickled back slowly. Owen remembered Cully

103

swinging that chair. He remembered throwing up his arm to ward it off. He didn't remember getting hit in the face. He tried to move his jaw and winced at the effort. It felt stiff and unwieldy, and just the thought of moving it sent waves of pain through his head.

Rockwood said, "I wired it while you were unconscious. First broken jaw I've had in a half-dozen years. Do you have a milk cow?"

Owen nodded. Molly had insisted upon one. He asked, "Where's Cully?" His voice came out a mumbling rasp.

Kilmonte frowned. "In jail. I'll take care of him."

Kilmonte had jumped to a conclusion. Owen didn't want Cully. Not now, at least.

Rockwood said, "You'll live on milk for the next thirty days. You'll hate the stuff before you're through."

Kilmonte said, "You worked him over pretty well, Owen. I came in just as he was swinging that chair. He hit you and pitched on his face, out cold. I dragged him to jail, and then Springman and I brought you here. Doc, if you're through with Owen, you might take a look at Cully. He needs some patching up."

Owen said, "Turn him loose." He was learning rapidly to be stingy with his words.

Kilmonte stared at him. "You're not preferring charges? Springman said he started it."

No, Owen thought. Cully didn't start it. Letty started it. Letty should be the one in jail.

"Turn him loose," he repeated.

Kilmonte made another wrong guess. "You leave him alone," he said brusquely. He looked at Owen and saw no malice in his eyes. Owen wasn't going after Cully. His eyes were puzzled as he said, "I won't hold him unless you say so."

Owen nodded. He wanted it that way. Maybe all of them had a part in the fault. And Cully was only a product of that faulting. And maybe that blow softened my head, Owen thought with bleak humor. But he couldn't feel any resentment toward Cully. Cully acted because of his sister. What will she do to Chad, Owen wondered. She's got a greater hold on him.

Kilmonte said, "I'll take Doc over to look at him. Wait here, and I'll drive you home."

Owen nodded. He was grateful to Kilmonte for the offer. He didn't feel like sitting a horse.

Rockwood paused at the door. "I'll take those wires out in a month. You treat that jaw gentle."

Doc didn't have to warn him. The pain did a thorough job.

Owen thought sourly, Doc Rockwood was right about one thing. He was sick of milk, and it took just three days. The throbbing pain in his face was gone, replaced by a great tenderness. A man didn't know how much he missed his mouth until it was wired shut.

He groaned as Molly came into the room with another pitcher of milk.

She said, "You've got to drink it. You'll fade away to nothing."

His jaws ached with the memory of steak, of solid food. He pointed to the table, telling her to put the milk down.

She asked, "How do you feel?" and he nodded in response. She asked him that a dozen times a day.

Enoch followed her into the room, and the old argument worked on his face. Enoch was outraged that Owen hadn't pressed charges against Cully.

Molly said warningly, "Let him alone, Enoch."

"Of all the damned foolishness," Enoch fumed. "We had a chance to even up with Derkses. And you tell Kilmonte to let Cully go."

Owen turned his face toward the window. Talking was a too difficult thing to waste it on arguing with Enoch.

That enraged Enoch, and he raised his voice. "You just show me where it makes any sense at all. You took all the punishment. It'll be easier for Cully to try it again."

No, Owen thought. Cully won't try it again. It took a combination of circumstances to bring the fight about, and Owen doubted that combination would happen again. Enoch was wrong about him taking all the punishment. Owen had done a little banging of his own on Cully.

Molly's temper was rising. "Let him be. You're at him every minute you're around." She pushed Enoch toward the door.

She closed it in Enoch's face and grimaced at Owen. "He's not a forgiving man."

Owen nodded agreement. It was surprising how much conversation a man could carry on with just a nod or a shake of his head.

She asked, "Do you need anything?"

He shook his head. He just wanted the slow, mending days to pass, and she couldn't do anything about that. He patted her arm in reassurance. He was doing fine.

He stared out of the window after she left. Inactivity was the worst disease of all. Molly would scream, but he was going to try some minor work this afternoon.

He stiffened as the two riders came into view, and his face hardened as he watched their approach. He had been thinking about Evlalie a good deal during the last few days. He had been thinking that by the end of the week he would ride over and see her. The trip would be unnecessary. She was riding to see him. And Clell Sawtelle was with her. He felt a grave wave of anger that was buried immediately by a following wave of loneliness. Evlalie wasn't riding here out of concern or anxiety for him. Hers was a duty call and nothing else. Proof of it was in the fact she had asked Sawtelle to come with her. Owen tried to keep the words from forcing their way into his mind, but he couldn't keep them out. She's made her choice. And that choice was Sawtelle.

He heard the door open, and he turned, his face carefully blank.

Molly came into the room, her face pleased. "Owen, Evlalie is coming. I wondered why she hadn't been over before."

He said a long sentence. "Maybe she had more important things to do."

Molly's eyes widened with surprise. "Now, Owen. Maybe she didn't hear about it, and—"

He said as savagely as his wired jaw would permit, "I don't want to see her."

Worry replaced Molly's surprise. She placed her hand on his arm. "Owen, you can't do that. What could I tell her?"

He jerked his arm from her touch. He would not sit and listen to Sawtelle make meaningless talk. He would not sit and watch Sawtelle's eyes stray to Evlalie every few seconds.

"Tell her I'm asleep." He turned his back on Molly. Molly would call him stubborn and childish, but she didn't know. No one could know unless they had the big, aching hurt of loneliness inside them. It was better to end it quick than to let it drag on with polite nothings. Molly wouldn't lie well. Evlalie would see that he did not want to see her. He wanted it that way, he wanted it ended right now.

"All right," Molly said crisply. "If that's the way you want it."

He did not answer her, and she slammed the door behind her.

He stared moodily at the far corner of the room until he heard the departing clop, clop, clop of the horses. He did not look out the window. The door on this phase of his life was closed. He would be foolish to open it even a crack to catch a glimpse of her.

Molly came back, and her eyes were angry. "You made a liar out of me. Evlalie knew I was lying."

He wanted to ask how Evlalie took it, was there hurt in her face, did she show care? He pushed those questions out of his mind and grunted a response.

"I hope you know what you're doing," Molly said. "Mark my words. Someday, you're going to regret this."

Molly was wrong, when she said someday. He was regretting it right now.

THIRTEEN

Cully's face still bore the marks of the fight three weeks after it had happened. His nose would never be straight again, and the cuts around his left eye would heal as scars. But the vivid color of the bruises was almost faded, and he could speak without swollen lips making his words grotesque.

Chad still felt uncomfortable being in the same room with him, as if it were some form of disloyalty toward his brother. But Owen had started the fight. Chad was positive of that. And Owen had been well on his way to beating Cully to pieces, until Cully hit him with the chair.

Nobody would talk to Chad about it. And he wouldn't ride home the word slipped into his mind before he could stop it— to get the facts. Cully wouldn't talk about it. He kept shaking his head and saying, "I'm not mad." He was a damned, odd Indian. Chad had never heard of one that couldn't hold a mad over a real or fancied hurt. There was no fancy about those marks on Cully's face. Chad knew Owen hadn't preferred charges. Didn't that sound as though Owen were the aggressor? Owen had a flash temper, gone as quickly as it arose. He must have thought it over after the fight, and to make atonement to Cully, had ordered Kilmonte to set him free.

Chad had seen Scotty in town last week, and Scotty had been coldly evasive. "It was Owen's fight," he said. "Ask him about it." He had fixed Chad with a hard stare. Something was on his mind. But he moved on without saying it.

Kilmonte was equally evasive. He said, "If Owen isn't pushing it, don't you be poking around in it. Let it lay." Then he said something that Chad hadn't figured out yet. "Every man picks his own road. And he has to do it mostly by himself."

Chad thought fretfully, nobody will talk to me about it. Except Letty. She had talked enough about it to last a lifetime. She had screamed at him that Owen had tried to kill her brother because she wouldn't let him lay his hands on her. Chad had wanted to yell at her, "It's a damned lie," but supposing it could be true. It looked to Chad as though Owen had been after her at the Fourth of July dance. Owen had danced with her several times, and he held her pretty close. Letty claimed she had to refuse to dance with him any more. When Chad asked her why she hadn't brought all this out before, she claimed she didn't want to make trouble. She had no such restraint stopping her now. What about Owen hitting you, she had asked triumphantly. Doesn't that prove something to you?

Chad didn't know. He couldn't remember much preceding the blow. Could Owen have been jealous and mad and taken out both in the blow? No, Chad thought, no. Owen wouldn't do that. But the little suspicions kept nagging. If those were Owen's reasons for hitting him, then the same reasons could be behind Owen's fight with Cully.

Chad thought morosely, you never really knew a person. You could live with them for years and still not know what went on inside them. Look how Enoch had followed Letty and watched her bathe. Chad clenched his hands so hard they hurt. He should have knocked Enoch's head off. He had heard old men were like that. When they couldn't do much else, they looked. Enoch's dirty, old eyes had gone over Letty's body. It wasn't too hard to believe that Owen had the same impulses. Chad knew how she affected him. Wasn't the same blood in all three of them?

He wished he had all the answers. All he could do was to take what meager facts he had and examine them. Every one of them was a finger pointing at Owen. He couldn't blame Cully for defending himself.

Chad sighed and blinked his eyes. He wished all these pounding thoughts would let him alone. His head ached, and he moved it cautiously for fear it would roll off his shoulders. He wasn't going to drink any more of Linus Derks' whiskey, no matter how much he shoved it at him. He felt lonely and depressed. But he wasn't weakening. His place was with Letty, and he wanted it that way. But it was kind of bad that things had turned out the way they had.

Linus Derks watched him with a sly, amused eye. Letty was tearing the boy to pieces. It had been hard to keep Cully from talking about the fight. Just the thought of it could put a fanatic gleam in Cully's eyes. But Linus had made him keep still about it, when Chad was around. The less Cully said about it, the more convinced Chad became that Owen was the aggressor. Letty did enough talking about it for everybody. She screamed at Chad all the time. As long as she had this kind of hold on Chad, Chad was going to be useful to Linus Derks one of these days.

Linus yawned and said, "How about supper, Letty?" That was another smart move on his part—offering to let Chad and Letty share his roof. He had made the offer a week ago, knowing that Chad was broke and would have to accept it. Enoch Parnell had thrown them out. Linus Derks gave them shelter. It put him a cut above Enoch.

Letty said sullenly, "All I do is cook and wash dishes for you three."

A nasty rejoinder was on Linus's tongue, and he swallowed it. It didn't matter a damn to him, whether Letty stayed or went. But he wanted Chad. Chad was going to be valuable.

Chad watched her, and the misery was plain in his eyes. She hated it here, and he couldn't blame her for that. But what could he do? He was broke and had no prospects of a job. He had tried to tell her that his low spot was only temporary, but she wouldn't listen. He didn't like it here, either, but he was grateful to Linus. His and Letty's bedroom was a blanket-partitioned corner of the room. Letty wouldn't let him touch her, saying fiercely she wasn't going to have Linus and Cully listening to and laughing at them. Chad knew he could get a job, if he wanted to leave her for a while. He guessed he was going to have to.

Letty moved to the stove, and her eyes smoldered as she looked at grease congealed in the frying pan. The few other pots and pans were dirty, and the water bucket was empty. A lone stick of wood was in the wood box.

The smoldering burst into flame, and she wanted to scream at all of them. They expected her to do everything. She picked up, the frying pan to carry it outside and clean it, then slammed it back on the stove. She couldn't stand any more. She was through.

She faced them, and her voice was shrill and harsh. "I'm leaving. I can do better than this. Pigs live better than we do."

Linus frowned. If it wasn't so far across the room, he would get up and belt her. Here he was feeding and sheltering her, and did she appreciate it? She did not. Letty never appreciated anything.

"I'll bet you can do better," he jeered.

Her body was a bowstring of fury. "I'll show you. I can support myself. Schober offered me a job in his restaurant. I can take the job anytime I want it."

Schober had offered the job, while she and Chad lived in town. She hadn't taken the offer seriously then, but now it had its appeal. She hadn't minded that little, rented room. She wouldn't mind living in it by herself. If she had to serve food all day long, at least, she would be paid for it.

Chad said violently, "I won't let you take it."

That pulled her attention to him. "How are you going to stop me?" she asked scathingly. He couldn't support her, and he still thought he had the right to tell her what to do.

She wanted to make him suffer, and she said, "Schober thinks I would draw business to his restaurant." She drew a deep breath, lifting her breasts. The misery in Chad's eyes made him look sick. He remembered, all right. He remembered a lot of things.

Linus said with cynical amusement, "You working?"

"I'll show you." Now that she had said it, she couldn't back down. She was frightened, but the defiance outweighed the fright. Anything was better than living here.

Chad watched her with those sick eyes. She would draw business to Schober's. He had no doubt of that. Men would come in to look at her. Their eyes would run over her, and they would laugh. Maybe she would join their laughter. And maybe Schober had something more in mind, when he offered her that job. Schober was a fat, old German, but old men could have thoughts, when it came to Letty. Chad had proof of that. He felt the rage knotting in his stomach. If Schober tried to touch her, he would kill him.

"Letty," he pleaded. "I'll get a job. We'll go anywhere you say."

She raked him with scornful eyes. "How long do you expect me to wait? The rest of my life?" The more she thought about it, the better she liked it. She was tired of Chad, tired of his constant begging. This was a way to end it, and she was going to take it.

"No," she said, shaking her head. "I'm leaving."

He jumped to his feet. "I'll go with you."

Her laughter was the cruelest sound he had ever heard. "You're not much of a man, are you, Chad? You'd go with me and expect me to support you. You'd live off me, wouldn't you?"

Chad turned deathly pale. "Go on," he said in a low voice. "But I'll be coming after you."

She laughed again. "You come after me, when you can support me. I won't hold my breath until you do."

She enjoyed all this. She was the center of the stage. Every moment belonged to her. She packed her few belongings, while they watched silently. She walked to the door, carrying the small bag.

She said, "And I don't need any of you to saddle a horse for me."

Linus watched Chad curiously. He had never seen a man need a woman this bad. It was a weakness he was glad he had never had. That weakness was a strong rope, binding Chad, and the end of it was in Linus Derks' hand.

He walked over to Chad and put a hand on his shoulder. "Let her go. She'll get sick of it soon enough. She'll get to missing you, and she'll be back. A smart man never chases after a woman."

Chad heard his voice but not the words. He was thinking of that good week he and Letty had in town, the week of his winning at the poker table. It could be like that again, if he had money.

He looked at his clenched hands. "I've got to get some money," he muttered.

Linus's eyes brightened with a wicked spark. When a man needed money as desperately as Chad sounded, there wasn't much he wouldn't do for it.

He said, "You just stick with me. I'll show you how to make money. More money than you ever had before." He had Chad's attention. Chad was looking at him, and Linus could see the hope in Chad's eyes. He hammered home the final rivet. "When you get that money, you'll see her change. You'll see how fast she comes back to you."

FOURTEEN

The hot, arid weather held well into September. The grass was long dead, and only a few dried wisps remained. Owen watched the weary, monotonous parade of days, and his worry grew. The high, summer range was going fast, and even if sufficient grass remained, the weather would drive the cattle from the mountains. It was going to be cold up there by the end of the month. What would they bring the cattle back to? The home range should have grown, while the cattle were off it, and it hadn't. They would bring the cattle back to scanty fall and winter pasture. He looked at the row of haystacks. They looked woefully small and terribly few in number.

Enoch was worried, too, though he tried to keep from showing it. It made him more silent, and when he did speak, his voice was testy. Owen learned not to talk to him unless Enoch spoke first. The silence touched Molly, making her face strained. She never mentioned Chad, though Owen knew she thought of him a lot. They had heard Chad and Letty were living with Linus Derks. Enoch had gone into a fearsome rage at the news. "He's picked his side," he raged. "Now he can rot with them."

No one could ever go back, but a man remembered the times that were better and longed for them. Owen remembered the times before Letty touched this house. There had been laughter at the table then. Maybe Enoch didn't join in, but he hadn't stopped it. That was gone. The laughter between Molly and her sons wouldn't touch this house again.

Owen and Enoch's last big argument had been the first of the month. Owen had begged Enoch to cancel the two thousand head of cattle coming in. Enoch had shouted, "You're asking me to go back on a contract? I couldn't cancel them, if I wanted to. They've been on the trail for six weeks. We'll pick them up at Miles City the fifteenth." He said warningly, "Don't bring it up again."

Owen rubbed his jaw. It was a habit formed during the long days it ached. It caused him no trouble now, though he wondered if the cold weather would bother it. Cold weather could play hell with a broken bone. Its icy fingers seemed to enter the old crack and spread an ache through the length of the bone.

Enoch said the new cattle would be here on the fifteenth. It's done, Owen thought. Nothing could change the road ahead of them.

Enoch took Owen and Les and Abel with him, when he rode to Miles City for the cattle. Hamp and Scotty were still in summer camp. It didn't leave enough men to handle a big herd, especially one strange to the range. When Owen pointed it out, Enoch snapped, "Don't you think I know that? I'll hire some men in town, or borrow a few drovers from the trail herd."

Owen grimaced. Those Texas drovers would love that. After weeks of trailing the herd this far, two or three more days of it would be a tremendous burden.

They rode into Miles City, and the cattle weren't there. Enoch fumed about it, though it wasn't that upsetting. It wasn't unusual for a trail herd to miss the delivery date by a few days.

"We'll stay the night," Enoch said.

Les and Abel were tickled. Owen wasn't. He hadn't been to town since his fight with Cully. He hadn't wanted to run into Cully again. It was a sincere effort to keep the peace, for if he had trouble again with Cully, he knew what he would do. He would kill the man. He didn't want to run into Chad or Letty, and he certainly didn't want to see Evlalie or Sawtelle. He had a long list of people he was avoiding, and if he kept adding to it, he might as well become a hermit. He grinned humorlessly at the thought.

Enoch said, "We'll eat at the hotel."

"I'm not hungry," Owen answered. He was going to eat, but not with Enoch. He had eaten enough meals with his father.

He walked down the street toward Schober's restaurant. Schober served fair food, though some of his dishes were foreign to Owen's taste.

He stepped inside and would have backed out, but it was too late. Letty had already seen him. She was laughing at some remark one of McLaughlin's cowboys made to her. Owen knew the man only as Red.

The laughter died as she looked at Owen. She looked Indian, when her face was impassive like that.

Owen moved to the counter and sat down. His pride wouldn't let him retreat with Red and Letty watching him.

Red scowled at him, and Owen wondered what he had interrupted. Red tried to catch Letty's attention again, but she was coolly inattentive to him. Red finished his meal and slammed payment on the counter. He had something on his mind to say to Owen. It showed in his indecisive pause, but he left without speaking. Owen let out a breath of relief. Letty bred trouble wherever she was.

She looked good. To a man, woman-starved by the long, monotonous hours of range work, she would look more than good. She was a lot of woman. Some other man might hold her, but Owen doubted Chad ever could.

She put a tentative smile on her face. "Owen, I'm glad to see you."

He gave neither the smile nor the words much value. She would greet most men like this. He asked, "Where's Chad?"

Sulkiness wiped out the smile. "How do I know." Enoch, Molly and Owen—they were all alike. That was where the trouble started. None of them thought of her. Their only concern was Chad.

Owen stared at her. She should know; she was Chad's wife.

She wanted to hurt him, and she said, "The last time I saw him he was drunk. Kilmonte threw him in jail."

Owen kept his wince hidden. "Letty, why don't you let him go?"

The question enraged her. "I don't want him. He keeps coming in here bothering me." Her passion mounted until her face was mottled with color. "None of you ever thought I was good enough for him."

115

Owen admitted the truth of her charge. He was seeking for words to calm her, when Schober, drawn by her loud voice, came out of the kitchen. He was a fat man, his round, full face crowned by a thin ring of white hair. It was hot in the kitchen, and sweat glistened on his face. He sized up the scene, and his face turned angry.

"Is this man bothering you?" he asked Letty.

"Yes," she said, a malicious spark in her eyes. "I was minding my own business, and he came in and insulted me."

Schober quivered with rage. "She is a good girl," he said pantingly. He had a heavy, German accent, and he made good sound like goot. "I will not have men like you bothering her. You get out now, or I will call the sheriff."

She was a confirmed liar. It was hard to prove an attractive woman a liar. Owen stood and walked to the door. He looked back, and she was laughing at him. He felt completely helpless. What weapons did a man use to fight a woman like her?

He moved to the corner of the block and rolled a cigarette. His face was heavy with somber reflection. Chad would learn someday, but before it happened, he was going to be badly mauled. He already has been, he thought gloomily.

He didn't know Kilmonte was near, until he spoke. "Did you talk to Letty?" Kilmonte asked.

So Kilmonte had seen him come out of the restaurant. The man didn't miss much of what went on in this town.

"Not much," Owen said.

Kilmonte fumbled in his vest pocket, and Owen handed him the makings. He waited while Kilmonte built his cigarette. Kilmonte had something to say, and he would say it in his own good time.

Kilmonte took a deep drag. "I arrested Chad last week."

"Why?"

"Drunk and disorderly," Kilmonte grunted. "He went into Schober's and tried to force Letty to go with him. Schober came screaming down the street after me."

"She's his wife."

That nettled Kilmonte. "It doesn't give him the right to do anything he damn pleases."

He waited for Owen's comment and received none. "Derks paid his fine the next morning." That should rap Owen.

Owen remained silent, but he hurt inside. Chad was getting pretty bound to Linus Derks.

Kilmonte took an angry draw and snapped the unfinished cigarette into the street. "I'm warning you, Owen. You'd better get Chad away from Derks. He's gone a long way downhill. He's heading for trouble."

Owen's anger broke. "You jump sides pretty quick, don't you? It wasn't too long ago that you were backing Derks."

Kilmonte's voice had a tired quality. "That was a different set of circumstances." Couldn't Owen see that a sheriff's job was to act on each set as they appeared? He said abruptly, "I've told you."

He turned and marched down the street.

Owen watched him until he turned the corner. He knew what Kilmonte was trying to do. He said silently, I can't do a thing about it, either, John.

The cattle didn't arrive the next day, and Enoch cursed about it. "A delivery date is a delivery date," he shouted. "Do they expect me to sit here the rest of the year waiting for them to get here?"

Owen said wearily, "Leave Les or Abel here. He can come after us, when the cattle arrive." He had work to do. He didn't want to sit around in this damned town another hour.

Enoch scowled at him. "I don't need you to think for me. I've already told Les to stay."

It delighted Les and made Abel unhappy. Enoch looked back at Abel and said, "Come on, Goddamn it. And get that long look off your face."

Les came after them a week later. "They're here," he said.

Enoch frowned. "How do they look?"

"Like hell." Les shook his head. "Some of them are standing and that's about all."

"Rest and a little feed will put them back in shape." Enoch sounded positive, but worry gnawed behind his eyes.

Oh sure, Owen thought. And where in the hell are you going to find that feed?

Bill Campbell was the trail boss. He was a tall, lanky Texan with a big, loose mouth. It was thin now as he looked at the herd with Owen and Enoch.

"Sixteen hundred head," he said, an angry snap in his voice. "I lost four hundred." The loss was an affront to his pride: "I never saw the trail so crowded. We were late getting started, and a half-dozen herds were ahead of us. They got all the grass."

This was a rainbow herd, of white and dun, roans and red. The red predominated, showing Durham blood. Les hadn't overstated it, when he said the cattle looked like hell. These animals were ganted, their ribs showing, their backbones a long razor's edge. Many of them were unsteady on their feet.

Owen listened to the clacking horns. This was a restless, hungry herd. And more cattle like these were pouring into Montana. They would keep coming up the trail until the weather closed down.

Enoch said, "I'll need a couple of men to get them to my range."

Campbell nodded moody agreement. He would make any concession to get his herd off his hands. "I hope you got some graze to throw them onto."

Enoch said stiffly, "We'll get by."

Owen wanted to yell at him. That "getting by" was a big, unanswered question. He thought fiercely, I'm glad for the loss. It was four hundred less seeking mouths to worry about.

FIFTEEN

By early fall, the Chicago market was quoting cattle prices at $3.90 a hundredweight, and the bottom was not in sight. A twelve hundred pound steer brought less than fifty dollars a head, and it cost six dollars to ship that steer to Chicago. Enoch no longer bellowed with rage at each new market report. His only outward sign now was a tightening of his mouth. In four years, cattle prices had dropped almost thirty-six dollars a hundred. The falling market was clubbing cattlemen to their knees, and still the cattle poured into Montana. The Miles City *Bulletin* said it was estimated a hundred thousand head were driven into Montana during the summer of '85. The E-P wasn't alone in fighting for its economic life.

All cattlemen rode in the same leaky boat, trying to bail it out with the teaspoon of lower market prices, while wave after wave of fixed or higher expenses washed over them. It might have been wiser to abandon the boat and swim for it, but the boat was the only thing they knew. So they clung to it, and the squeeze between return and outgo became more vicious. The economic squeeze would have been bad enough, but the weather added its crushing weight. The fall rains didn't appear, and the grass remained brown and lifeless. Even a brief greening up would have been welcome, an inch of new growth, anything.

To the eyes of a poet, the fall was beautiful. The canyons and coulees were a riot of color. Nature splashed her paintpots recklessly over groves of golden quaking aspens, orange cottonwood, and scarlet thornbushes. The crimson rose briars and trailing clematis with its white cotton balls intermingled with the evergreen of pine, fir, and spruce.

A cattleman didn't have a poet's eye. Cattle couldn't eat that flaming color. Green was the color the cattleman wanted, the green of grass.

Scotty rode up to Owen and asked, "You got the makings? I must have lost mine someplace."

Owen handed him papers and a sack of tobacco. He watched a bead of sweat form at the crown of Scotty's nose, run the length of it, and drop off. Scotty's weariness showed in the drawn lines of his face. We're all tired, Owen thought, but Scotty showed it the most. He was almost Enoch's age, and the long hours in the saddle were demanding their toll. The damned new cattle, Owen thought with a quick rage. They would not settle down. They drifted all over the range, and E-P riders were kept busy turning them back at the passes. Sufficient graze might have stabilized them, but there wasn't sufficient graze, and Owen swore the new animals shuffled around bawling more than they looked for grass. The old herd was northern grown range stock, familiar with range and conditions. They adapted instead of wandering restlessly about.

Scotty handed back the makings. "Think we'll ever get them settled down?" He looked at a dozen cows, a hundred yards away. They stood with their heads up, their mouths open with their bawls of protest. "Goddamn Texas cattle," he said in sudden rage. "What do they do down there? Carry their feed out to them?"

Owen started to say something and stopped as the faint cry drifted down from overhead. He threw back his head and looked. High in the sky was the long, perfect V of the flock of geese. The cry of the wild goose always stirred him. It had a sweet sadness to it, and it pulled at earth-bound man. It made him restless and discontented with his lot, it made him wish he was as free as the wild geese.

Scotty was watching the geese with the same rapt attention. It was a rare man who didn't throw back his head when the wild goose called.

Scotty said, "That's the third bunch I've seen today. They're going through pretty early."

Owen nodded. The ducks were flying, too. Scotty was right about it being early. Owen couldn't remember a year when the ducks and geese headed south this soon.

Scotty said, "They know. We're going to have an early and hard winter."

Owen was afraid Scotty was right. The horses were getting shaggier, and there seemed to be a mass migration of animals and birds toward the south, creatures that ordinarily wintered here. It was hot today, and tomorrow promised more of the same. But the wild creatures knew. They had some instinct that gave them foresight, where man was blind.

Scotty said, "I've been having the damnedest dream, Owen. I've dreamed it a dozen times. I'm riding all alone and all I can see is snow. Snow everywhere I look. I'm trying to get out of it, and a voice keeps saying, 'Scotty, you'll never see another spring.' I wake up then, and I swear I'm shivering."

He grinned with embarrassment. "I'm going to have to quit eating Les's cooking. It's souring my stomach."

Owen's outward disinterest helped Scotty cover his embarrassment. That dream bothered Scotty. It bothered him enough so that he had to tell somebody about it.

Owen grunted and rubbed his shoulder against his wet cheek. "Today, I wouldn't mind a little snow."

"We'll get it soon enough," Scotty said quietly.

That dream's hit him hard, Owen thought. He's afraid of it. He abandoned his search for the right words. Anything he said would only embarrass Scotty further.

Enoch yelled at him from a high point of ground. He was too far away for Owen to catch the words. He put his horse in motion, galloping toward Enoch. He looked back, and Scotty was motionless, his face turned toward the now empty sky. Animals had foresight. Did man sometimes have a glimmer of foresight, too? The wind was still hot, but Owen shivered.

Linus Derks came back from the door and said, "Ducks and geese going through." Satisfaction was in his tone. It meant an early winter. It meant they could get to work.

Chad mumbled something and reached for the whiskey bottle. These days, he remained in a state of drunkenness. It was easier this way, it kept a man from thinking. He hadn't shaved for a week, or changed his clothes for a longer period. He took a long pull at the bottle and shuddered. A man would never be able to get used to the whiskey Derks made.

Linus's eyes were filled with wicked satisfaction. In the past weeks, he had watched the dissolution of a man. Here was one of the high and mighty Parnells, pulled down about as low as a man could get. He wished Enoch Parnell could see his son now. He had been wrong in thinking Letty was useless to him. She had handed him Chad, and Chad was going to be valuable. Every time Chad came back from town he was either raving from anger or whiskey. The last two times, it had been only the whiskey. Letty's indifference was pounding the anger from him, leaving a helpless despair.

Linus felt only contempt for him. No real man would let a woman wreck him this way. Enoch called me a squaw man, he thought. By God, Chad's worse than I ever was. I never went wild, when I got a taste of that Indian blood.

He rubbed his hands and said, "Yes, sir, we'll be going to work pretty quick one of these days."

Chad turned dull eyes toward him. "It's about time," he mumbled. "I'm not sitting around here much longer." An inner eagerness burned through the whiskey fog in his eyes. "Can we make money skinning wolves, Linus?"

Linus nodded solemnly. "Good money. We've got to wait for a freeze, though. Then you'll have enough money to get anything you want."

Chad nodded with drunken heaviness. He'd show her. He'd come to her with his pockets filled with money. She'd be glad to see him, then. Maybe he would take her back, and maybe he wouldn't. Loneliness and the cruel need of her was an aching knot in his belly. He couldn't lie, even to himself. He'd take her back without another thought.

He pointed an unsteady finger at Linus. "I've waited a long time," he said. "If you've been lying to me—" The rest of the threat faded as he reached for the bottle.

Linus turned back to the door. The threat meant nothing to him. The big birds knew. When the geese started flying, it meant winter was close behind them. A long, bad winter could be ahead. He didn't mind. He'd come through long, bad winters before. He wasn't lying to Chad about making money killing wolves. They could pick up a few dollars, and more if they wanted to devote the entire winter to it. He had known of some wolfers making as much as twenty-five hundred dollars a season. But it was hard, dirty work, and a wolfer knew exposure and privation and danger. He did not intend to stay at it the entire winter. Not when there was a much easier, quicker way of getting that money. That was where Chad would come in handy. Chad could go on E-P range without Enoch blowing him full of holes.

SIXTEEN

A mountain of firewood was beside the kitchen door, and still Owen wasn't satisfied. He spent all the time he could, hauling in more logs, then chopping and splitting them into stove length.

Enoch growled, "You've got enough there to last us twenty winters."

Owen swung the ax, and the twelve-inch pine block split cleanly through the middle. "Maybe," he grunted. He upended one half, then split it into quarters. He vented his worry on the inoffensive logs. A dread picked at him, never letting him rest at ease. It was as bad as Scotty's dream. Worse, for its little claws raked at him both waking and sleeping hours.

He glanced at the sky. It was clear, but there was a leaden color to it that oppressed him. He could almost imagine the gray, winter clouds massing below the northern horizon. The heat was broken, and the wind had shifted to the north. It was more of a breeze than a wind, but it had a chilling quality to it.

Enoch said, "Everybody in this outfit goes around looking at the sky with a long face. Even Molly goes to the door a dozen times a day to look at it. Are you all wishing bad weather on us?"

Owen said quietly, "The ducks and geese are gone. The other birds are leaving. A lot of the wild animals are moving south, animals that usually stay here."

Enoch's face had a grim, stubborn set. "I don't give a damn. I've been on this range long enough to know its winters. We don't get snow or cold weather until after the first of the year. We had a bad summer. It won't be followed by a bad winter."

Owen set up another block to split. No one got anyplace arguing with Enoch. Enoch was talking about a normal year. It hadn't been normal since its start.

He heard Enoch leave and didn't turn his head. He hoped Enoch was right. He hoped desperately he was right. He went on splitting wood. He could have pointed out other signs to Enoch. The horses' shaggy coats of hair, the heavier coats on the cattle. Nature put a built-in wisdom and protection into her dumb things. Enoch would have denied those signs. He would also have denied that range conditions were changed. But they were. The thick brush and the tall rye grass, that used to exist along the streams and breaks, were gone, or fenced off by the nesters. The rye grass used to afford winter food and shelter. There was also the increase in cattle numbers, maybe by as much as three times. Enoch blinded himself deliberately to those things, then was furious, when other people worried. The ax blade rose and fell in a flashing arc of light much faster than a few moments ago. Owen had a sudden, explosive need for outlet.

The wind awakened Owen during the night. It had force that rocked the house, and he lay there, listening to it. The wind sound was a mournful, rising wail, and its icy fingers found tiny cracks in the house and filled Owen's room with a depressing weight on the temperature. The single blanket wasn't enough, and he lay shivering, half asleep and dreading to get up to get another blanket. He turned his head at footsteps outside the door.

Molly came into the room, carrying a lamp and another blanket. She spread the blanket over him, and it was one of the heavy, winter ones. She said, "I got them out yesterday and aired them."

She wore her winter robe and as she bent to kiss his cheek he saw her shiver. "You'd better get back to bed," he said.

"Owen, this storm is early, isn't it?"

"Yes," he said gruffly. It was the sixteenth of November. "It'll blow itself out in an hour or two." He hoped he was convincing.

He waited until she reached the door, then asked, "Is Enoch awake?"

"He's awake. He hasn't said anything. But he's awake."

So Enoch was listening to it, too. There had to be a dread in him, a dread that warred with his stubbornness. Owen hoped Enoch was hurting.

The door closed behind Molly. Owen wanted to be first up in the morning. He wanted to build a roaring fire and have the kitchen warm before she arose. The warmth of the extra blanket was a pleasant thing, but still sleep was a long time returning. The room was getting colder, and the wind buffeted the house in steady, successive blows, its voice roaring in wild abandon. During the brief lulls, Owen thought he heard little, peppering noises as if someone were throwing handfuls of gravel against the walls. It sounded like hail. He hoped not. He didn't want ice or snow now. He ducked his head under the blankets, and the increasing warmth made him drowsy. He drifted off to sleep, thinking of those Texas cattle. They had never known a storm as bad as this one sounded. They would be bawling their protest and drifting before the force of the wind.

It was still dark, when he awakened in the morning. His teeth chattered as he dressed. The wind was still up. He put on heavier socks, and the chill of his boots drove through them, until the heat of his blood drove it back. He moved to the kitchen and built a fire in the stove, standing with his hands over the iron top until the first small push of heat reached them. The crackling of the flames was a pleasant thing to hear, but with his other ear, he listened to the storm. He grunted as he thought of him telling Molly it would blow itself out in an hour or two.

The wood box was almost full, but he decided to bring in another armload. He really wanted to see how bad it was outside. He slipped into a heavy mackinaw, hanging on the peg. Molly must have put it there after supper last night. Molly had an instinct of her own.

He stepped outdoors and gasped. With a wind driving it, cold turned into a knife, slashing through a man's clothing and numbing his flesh. The earth was white, and he cursed that whiteness. He moved to the woodpile, his boots crunching against the snow. Icy particles still rode the wind, stinging his face until water rose to his eyes. He turned his face against it and walked to the lee side of the woodpile. It was only a degree better here. He gathered an armload of wood and turned back toward the house. The distance back seemed several times longer.

Just this short exposure numbed his hand, and he fumbled

with the knob. Someone opened the door for him, and he stepped inside. The water in his eyes momentarily blinded him, and his face felt raw and stinging. He groped his way to the wood box and deposited his armful of sticks. The healed jaw seemed aflame, and he rubbed his knuckles against it, trying to restore circulation.

Enoch asked, "How bad is it?"

He had eyes. He could see the raw, red look of Owen's face, the white coating on his mackinaw. "See for yourself," Owen said curtly. Enoch wasn't responsible for the storm, but Owen's tone sounded accusing.

Enoch scowled but didn't move from the stove. His heavy thoughts burdened his face.

Owen took off the mackinaw. Its white covering looked more like frost rime than snow. He shook the mackinaw and caught one of the white crystals in his hand. It had substance as if it actually were made of frosted glass. With these crystals riding a wind, no wonder a man's face stung.

The hands trooped in just as Molly was finishing breakfast. Since Letty and Chad left, the men ate in the kitchen with the family. Enoch had protested against it, but Molly insisted. Owen thought she welcomed the opportunity of hearing a cheerful word.

Seven people sat around the table, eating silently. In the middle of a bite, one would stop chewing, and his head would cock to the noise of the storm. The others watched him, and each head was filled with the same thought. What was happening to the cattle?

Scotty said, "I never saw anything like it in my days. I like to froze to death just making it here. My feet aren't warm yet."

The stove threw out a small circle of heat. It didn't quite reach to the table. Owen's feet were cold by the time breakfast was finished.

The men stood, and Molly saw their intent. "You're not going out now," she cried. "What can you do?"

"We can try," Owen said simply. "I'll bring in some more wood before I leave."

"I can get it."

"You stay inside." His tone was sharp. His face softened as he moved her out of the blast of the opening door. "Molly, this is a real bad one." He looked back and said, "We'll be back as soon as we can."

THE LONG COLD WIND

He had to take off his gloves to cinch up the saddle. The leather was stiff, and the hole seemed too small for the tongue of the buckle. His hands were numb by the time he had the gear on his horse. He heard swearing all around him. The horses were reluctant to leave the shelter of the barn, and they had to be dragged out.

"Star," Scotty yelled. "If you don't quit dragging back on me, I'll break your damned neck." He glanced at Owen and tried to grin. His stiffened lips failed to respond. "That horse is smarter than we are," he said. "He'd stay in, if he had the choice."

Owen wondered if Scotty were still bothered by his dream. Would Scotty stay inside, if he had the choice? Scotty would be indignant, if he knew the question was in Owen's mind. He had one choice, of his own making: the cattle.

They mounted and headed south, putting the wind at their backs. The cattle would drift before the wind, until they found shelter in some coulee or break, or were stopped by a barbed-wire fence. There, if the exposure lasted too long, they would die.

Owen couldn't hear the crunch of the horses' hoofs, but he knew the sound was there, swallowed by the greater sound of the wind. He judged three inches of the white, frozen crystals were already on the ground. It wasn't exactly sleet, but that was the closest he could come to it. He could feel its stinging against his back through his clothes. It would be hell riding against that stuff.

He pulled his scarf up, protecting his nose and ears, leaving only his eyes exposed. When he blinked them, the eyelids seemed heavy, and he thought the white crystals were freezing on his lashes.

They made a ghostly cavalcade riding through the weak light of the early morning. Enoch was only a dozen yards ahead of Owen, and at times, the swirling blasts of the sleet hid him.

Owen didn't know how far they had ridden. He hadn't seen a familiar landmark in the last hour. In this storm, distance was impossible to estimate, and a mile seemed like ten. He felt a lonely uneasiness. A man could lose all sense of direction. He could wander in this bleak, frozen world until he froze to death.

He swore at himself for the uneasy fancy. He was cold and miserable, but he wasn't alone. All they had to do to find their way back was to put the wind in their faces. They couldn't miss the house and outbuildings.

He recognized the break as they approached its lip. That gnarled tree, standing beside the bald rock, was a distinctive landmark. Cattle should be seeking shelter in the break. He saw the huddled animals, not fifty yards away, pressed tight against the near bank. The cutting wind howled over them, and the drifting sleet was piling up against the far side of the break. The cattle bawled plaintively at the sight of the riders, but none of them moved.

Owen judged there were forty cows and short yearlings in that bunch. He thought they were the old cows, familiar with this range. When the storm broke, they would head instinctively for the nearest shelter. None of the Texas cattle seemed to be in the bunch.

"I'd knew they'd find shelter. They're going to come through all right." The scarf muffled Enoch's voice, but it sounded jubilant.

He's worrying hard, Owen thought. He could point out that it was pretty early for jubilation. Forty head was only a tiny fraction of the E-P cattle.

Enoch moved off, and they followed him. It was a long and searching morning, probing for the weakness in a man, pounding him with merciless cold and pelting sleet until the marrow of his bones ached. Owen knew now what cold weather would do to his jaw. It ached with dull, clubbing blows. He tried to ignore it. It was going to be a long day and a longer winter. It was hard to ignore a persistent ache.

They found other bunches of cattle, and each time Enoch's assurance mounted. The cattle were miserable with the cold, but all of them had found some semblance of shelter and seemed to be in fair enough condition.

"They'll make it," Enoch said after sighting each bunch.

Wait, Owen kept thinking. Just wait. They still hadn't seen any of the Texas cattle. That was a big worry. Why hadn't those Texas cattle drifted to shelter along with the E-P cows?

An hour later, they found six of the Texas cattle. The gale was piling the snow into glacial drifts, and the six animals had stumbled into a drift reaching higher than their bellies. They were just standing in the drift, their heads down, too exhausted to struggle farther, or even to bawl.

Enoch tried to reach them, and his horse broke through the crust, sinking to the knee joint. Owen saw him rein out of the drift and head back. He joined him, and Enoch pointed at the horse's forelegs. Both of them showed the bright color of fresh blood.

"Don't put the horses in there," Enoch yelled. "When a horse breaks through the crust, it cuts like a knife." He swung down to inspect his horse's injuries, and Owen followed him. The cold was slowing the bleeding, and Enoch wiped his glove across one of the cuts. "It's sheared deep," he muttered. "Almost to the bone." He looked at Owen with anguished eyes. "I never saw anything like this before."

Owen nodded. He was thinking of the trip back. If a horse stepped into several drifts like Enoch's mount had, its legs could be cut so badly it would be useless. A man afoot out here wouldn't last very long.

"Enoch," he said. "We'd better be turning back."

"No," Enoch said. "I'm going to get those cows out."

They tried. They went on foot, hoping to drive the cows ahead of them, and the broken crust was sharp enough to cut clothing. They sank in higher than their waists, and a man trembled with fatigue after twenty steps. They yelled at the cows until they were hoarse, and the cows didn't even lift their heads.

Even stubborn, old Enoch was finally convinced they couldn't drive the animals out of the drift. Owen saw the droop of his shoulders as he turned and plowed out of the drift. Enoch never looked at the cattle again. It would have been kinder to shoot them. The animals would stand there, imprisoned by the mounting drift, until they froze to death.

Enoch mounted and turned his horse to the north. He rode with his chin on his chest, and it wasn't solely to protect his face from the blast. He was tired and cold and frightened. He saw something, something that Owen had been looking at for months. He had a right to his fright.

Owen saw the group of horsemen coming toward them first. He said warningly, "Enoch," and Enoch lifted his head.

Some of the old defiance straightened Enoch's back. What was this group of horsemen doing on his range?

It was hard to be sure how many there were until the intervening distance was lessened. The swirling snow made their forms ghostly, and a man got a different number every time he counted.

Less than a hundred yards were between them, when Owen was sure of the count. Six horsemen were in the party.

"Indians," he said, and pulled up and waited. He fumbled off a glove and pulled the rifle from its scabbard. He didn't think a raiding party would be out in this storm, but it was never wise to take a chance with Indians.

The group stopped thirty yards away, and one of them broke off and moved to Enoch and Owen. Cree, Owen thought. From north of the river. The man was muffled in blankets until only his eyes were uncovered.

The man threw up his hand, palm out. Owen put away the rifle. "Heap cold," the Indian said.

Owen nodded.

The man said something in Cree that Owen missed. He used a mixture of English and Indian, and it was hard to follow him.

"What are they doing here?" Enoch asked impatiently.

"Where you go?" Owen asked, falling into the patois.

The Indian pointed vaguely toward the south. "Family move. Too cold."

Owen looked at the two older people, grandparents, he judged, at the patient, huddled squaw, at the two children in their teens. South was only a general direction. This family had a long way to go to get out of this.

"You got whiskey?" the Indian asked eagerly.

Owen shook his head, and there was regret in the gesture. This was one time he would give whiskey to the Indians. Today, whiskey would be a fuel instead of strong drink. It would pump fire along icy veins, it would sweep life-giving heat through numbed flesh.

"No whiskey," he said.

The Indian sighed. "We go," he said. His next sentence was a long one, of English and Indian words.

Owen caught something about white owls and wise Indian, he move as fast as he can.

"What's he saying?" Enoch asked.

Owen shook his head. "I'm not sure." He wished he could tell the Indian about the six cows held in the drift. He wished he could say, go ahead. Butcher one or all of them. But even if the Indians could find the animals in this trackless waste, Enoch would never stand for it. He would call it encouraging them to steal again.

"We go," the Indian said again and drew his blankets more tightly about him. "Kissin-ey-oo-way'-o," he said softly.

Owen had heard the phrase before. It meant, it blows cold. The Crees were people from the top of the land, land gripped most of the year by cold. They were used to cold, and when they fled before it, it was something to worry about.

The Indian party filed past them and were swallowed by the curtain of white in less than two hundred yards. They would make it, if any people could.

Enoch said fretfully, "I hope this storm doesn't drive all of them down on us. They'll steal everything they can get their hands on."

Owen started to say something, and a startled croak from Scotty stopped him. Scotty pointed at a flock of birds that materialized suddenly and were gone as quickly. But Owen got a good look at them. They were big birds, snow-white with rounded heads and huge, baleful, staring eyes. Now he knew what the Indian had been trying to say. The great white owls of the Arctic were here. He had seen pictures of them, but they rarely came this far south. An occasional old-timer spoke of having seen them. They always wound up by saying, "When you see the white owls, find yourself a deep cave and don't come out until spring. Because you're going to catch hell."

Owen's face was sober. Montana was a long way south of the Arctic. It took the worst kind of weather to drive the owls this far. Kissin-ey-oo-way'-o, he repeated silently. He wasn't sure he could pronounce it. He wasn't even sure he had all the syllables in it. But he agreed with its meaning.

He looked at Scotty. Scotty was shivering violently. He hadn't been shivering before the owls appeared.

SEVENTEEN

The storm blew itself out in two days. Linus Derks opened the cabin door and looked at the sky. The night was clear, the stars shining. But they shone with a cold glitter, and the white-covered earth threw back that glitter. The air was thin and sharp with cold. Linus shivered. He judged the temperature to be near zero. It would drop much lower before morning.

It was a quiet cold, unlike the bluster of the last two days. This cold crept up a man and before he knew it, his flesh was numb. But this was the kind of weather he had been waiting for. He didn't care how many storms happened during the winter just as long as they were followed by a period of relatively better weather.

"Shut that door," Cully yelled. "You trying to freeze us out?"

Linus shut the door and turned. He glared at Cully, then at Chad. He was sick of both of them. Another day of confinement in this cabin would have all of them at each other's throat. Cully and Chad were half drunk, and they wrangled constantly. Twice, Linus had to prevent them from coming to blows. Maybe he should let them knock each other around. Maybe it would blunt the sour edge of their dispositions.

He glanced at the wood box, and it was nearly empty. He said, "We'll run out of wood before morning." Cutting wood was a simple chore, but the two griped about it as if he were asking for their blood. They even expected him to cut and bring in his share. By God, he was the head of the house. That entitled him to a few privileges. Besides, wasn't he feeding and sheltering them? Add up all the whiskey they drank, and they'd run up quite a bill.

Cully said, "It's about time you cut your share."

Linus said, "You can freeze, for all I care." He turned toward his bed. He had the only two extra blankets in the cabin. The others were hidden in the shed. They could lie and shiver until one of them grew cold enough to bring in more wood.

He pulled off his boots and crawled under the blankets. He grunted with animal comfort as the pleasant warmth stole through his body.

He said, "We start early in the morning. You'd better get some sleep."

Neither seemed to hear him. They were arguing over the last drink in the bottle. Linus knew a sudden, vicious rage. He was sick of both of them. The next three weeks would knock some of that smartness out of them. He'd work them until they dropped. He fell asleep with the pleasant thought.

He awakened them before light in the morning. The cabin was cold, and the wood box was empty. He wanted a hot cup of coffee, but he could forgo it in the joy of watching them suffer. Both of them carried big heads, and they moved with caution as though they were afraid a jar would break the thin string holding their heads to their bodies.

"I'll cut some wood," Cully said. He said it with reluctance, his eyes hopeful that someone would argue with him.

"I could stand some coffee," Chad grunted.

Linus's eyes gleamed with satisfaction. Their repayment was starting. "We haven't time," he said.

Chad's face turned stubborn. "I'm not going anywhere until I get some coffee."

Linus lunged at him and slammed the heel of his palm into Chad's chest. The blow knocked Chad into a wall. He bounced off it, and for an instant, the old angry spark flashed in his eyes.

Linus watched him, wondering if he had misjudged his timing. A month ago, he wouldn't have dared slam into Chad like that. The whiskey and the loneliness were small hatchets, chopping away at Chad's moral fiber. Had they chopped enough?

The spark in Chad's eyes faded. He was sick with the aftereffects of whiskey, he was cold and miserable. He hadn't been hurt. It wasn't worth fighting about.

Linus let out his breath. He hadn't misjudged a thing. He said, "We got work to do."

He wouldn't have any more trouble with Chad. Men broke under various stresses, and Linus wondered briefly why the breaking point in men varied so much. He shrugged and let go of the thought. He was only interested in whether or not a man was useful to him   not how he got that way.

He picked up an armload of supplies from the floor and Chad and Cully followed suit. Three pack horses and three saddle horses were in the ramshackle structure that replaced the shed. One corner of it sagged perilously. Linus had thought a dozen times they should get out there and strengthen the structure.

The load could have been put on one pack animal, but Linus distributed it among the three. He hoped their luck was good enough to load all three pack animals with wolf pelts.

He checked everything that went into the packs. He had flour, beans, sugar, coffee, and salt. A monotonous fare was ahead of them. He packed a pair of blankets, and a buffalo robe for each man. He checked to be sure he had plenty of ammunition for the rifles and pistols. Indians hated wolfers. They lost so many dogs to the poisoned bait wolfers put out. But they respected a good rifle and kept their distance. The Indians would be looking at three good rifles. But the bastards could hit in other ways than a direct attack. They could cut up and destroy the skins or steal a wolfer's horses, putting him afoot. In below zero temperatures, that meant certain death. They wouldn't put Linus Derks afoot, not with one man always standing guard.

The hunting knives were long and sharp. Linus had honed the edges yesterday. He was meticulous about the packing of the strychnine, wrapping it several times and packing it on one of the animals that didn't carry food. The stuff was deadly, and he didn't want any of its white crystals spilling into anything he ate.

He made a final inspection and was satisfied. He intended to stay out three weeks. He had supplies for longer than that, and most wolfers took to the plains with the first freeze and did not return until spring. But three weeks should be enough to open Chad's eyes.

THE LONG COLD WIND

He mounted and led a pack horse. Chad and Cully followed him. The light was just getting strong as they started. It would be cold even after the sun came up. At this time of year, the sun's rays were pretty watery.

Skinning wolves was cold, dirty work, and a man suffered under its privations. It could also be profitable. Linus wanted Chad to go into town with money in his pocket. Letty could always hear the voice of money. When that voice faded, Chad would have a choice to make—of returning to the dirty business of gathering more pelts, or making his money much easier and faster. Linus didn't think there was any doubt which course Chad would choose.

He thought about wolves as he rode. He knew a great deal about them. The big, gray timber wolf was a smart animal. He was fast, and he had unlimited endurance. It was hard to get a shot at one and equally hard to trap them. The wolf had a lot of cunning and a ferocity to direct that cunning. But strychnine could get them. They paired up and whelped in the summer. Linus had seen as many as ten pups in a den. In the summer, the wolf pairs lived on small game such as fawns and rabbits. But with the coming of freezing weather, their appetites grew ravenous. They banded together, hunting for bigger game. As many as thirty wolves were in a pack under the leadership of a smart old dog captain. Linus was positive that wolves could communicate with each other. When the buffalo was plentiful, he had watched a dog captain direct his pack. The pack followed the buffalo herd, keeping near the cows and calves, waiting for a small bunch to become detached from the main herd. The pack separated into three groups, one group slipping in between the main herd and the detached small bunch. The second group, under the leadership of the captain, drove straight for the head of the selected cow. The third group moved in behind her, cutting off possible retreat. Being almost surrounded, she could only stand and make a fight of it. Usually the dog captain sprang for her muzzle. If his slashing teeth missed, the others were right behind him. The cow couldn't face in two directions at once. While she tried to keep those cruel teeth from cutting her muzzle to ribbons, the rear group slipped up and hamstrung her. A buffalo cow didn't stand much chance. Wolves pulled her down in a hurry.

Cattle herds were even easier for wolves. Cattle were afraid of them and ran in a straight line at the sight of one. Wolves had more endurance and were faster than cattle. It wasn't hard for them to drag down a range animal. Cows would try to protect their calves, but a cow was no match for even a lone wolf, not when that wolf weighed from a hundred and twenty-five to a hundred and fifty pounds.

Linus respected wolves. They were adapted to live in a hard country, and they made it well. They had one weakness, a consuming appetite for animal fat. They couldn't resist a bacon rind liberally smeared with lard. The lard was laced with strychnine crystals.

A wolfer earned every dollar he made. He lived under the harshest of conditions, and if the Indians didn't ruin his pelts, a sudden thaw could. A cattleman prayed for a chinook, the wolfer dreaded them. Linus looked at Chad's and Cully's moody faces. They had a hard day ahead of them. By night, all the whiskey fumes would be worked out of them.

He showed Chad how to mix the strychnine crystals into the lard, warning him to be careful not to get any on his hands. If a man touched his eyes with strychnine on his fingers, it could have serious effects. Though he had never witnessed it, Linus had heard tales of men going blind because of rubbing the poison into their eyes. It was a poison and deadly, and he gave it the respect it deserved.

They crossed the southwest corner of E-P land. Even if old Enoch found them, he shouldn't do more than grumble. They were wolfers and could prove it. Cattlemen approved of wolfers. Every wolf carcass meant a corresponding save in the spring calf crop.

In a little break in the land, they found six cows frozen to death in a drift. Some attempt had been made to save those cows. Linus saw horse tracks, and the wallowing where a man had attempted to breast the drift. The first cold spell of the winter had pinched Enoch Parnell. The wolves had been here, too. The crust of the snow was too hard to take their impressions, but those torn-out sides of the cows could mean only wolves.

Chad stared soberly at the dead animals, and Linus wondered what he was thinking. It was hard to break the bondage of years of association and blood, and probably some small tie still remained. Linus expected that. But before too many weeks passed, he thought that last small tie would snap.

He started setting out the baits at the dead cows. He laid them out in a big circle, extending far onto the plain. By nightfall, he judged they had covered better than twenty miles. Tomorrow, they would ride back over those miles and garner what the poison had killed.

The stars were bright and cold. Linus saw no evidence of a chinook. He judged this present cold snap would hold for a week or more.

They found shelter in a coulee and ate a drab meal, huddled around a small fire. After the meal, Cully pawed through the supplies.

"If you're looking for the whiskey, I took it out," Linus said. He saw the meanness harden both faces and said, "You'll get no drink until we finish out here."

He unbuttoned his coat and laid his hand on the pistol butt as the two exchanged glances. If they were foolish enough to try to jump him, he'd stop them. Chad first, then Cully. He said calmly, "Get that damned fool notion out of your heads."

He saw the resistance spill out of them. The rebellion was over. It might flare again, but it would be weaker next time. He rolled up in his blankets and laid down on half the buffalo robe, pulling the other half over him. A man had to guard as much against the cold stealing up from the ground as the cold in the air. He felt snug and cozy, and he was going to sleep well. Let Chad and Cully sit at that fire all they pleased. They'd roast their front and freeze their behind. They'd get enough of that in a hurry.

He had them awake early. They had a lot of miles to ride, and if luck was with them, a great deal of work to do. Chad and Cully moved as though they hurt, and Linus grinned sardonically. Take whiskey away from a man who's been on a pretty steady diet of it, and he suffered.

They found twenty-six dead wolves, the bodies frozen stiff. Chad was awkward and slow with the skinning, and Linus kept saying, "Goddamn it. Watch. Like this." Chad gave him a bleak look and bent to his work.

By nightfall, he was sick of it. He couldn't use the knife well with gloves on, and without them, his hands ached with the cold. The smell of wolf carcasses filled his nostrils and coated his mouth. He tasted it with his evening meal. Linus said they would be out three weeks. Chad wasn't sure he could take twenty more days of this.

Linus grinned at the broody look on Chad's face. Maybe it

wouldn't take three weeks to give him a full belly of this. Maybe he would get smart in less time.

Just before dark, they had passed a bunch of a dozen E-P horses. Horses fared better in winter than cattle. If the earth was snow-covered, horses would paw down through it to find feed. Chad had pointed out a sorrel and said, "I watched him grow up. I broke him." A kind of longing was in his voice. Chad belonged with horses. Linus intended that was just where he would be.

They loaded the pack animals with wolf pelts in sixteen days, sixteen hard, monotonous days, sixteen days without seeing the inside of a man-made shelter. Chad thought he must have skinned a million wolves, and the smell was permanently ground into him. He felt crawling with dirt, and the thick beard stubble itched his face. His clothing was stiff with dried blood. He wanted a bath and fresh clothing. He wanted to see Letty again. The ache in his belly sprang to life.

"How much will they bring?" he asked Linus.

Linus shook his head dubiously. "That depends on a lot of things. I'll take them to the trading post at Fort Benton and see."

"Let's get going," Cully said. Those sixteen days had galled Cully, too. He was ready for town and a spree.

Linus shook his head. "You go back to the cabin and wait for me." At the black look spreading over Cully's face he shouted, "You can wait a few more days, can't you. Miles City has more to offer than Fort Benton, doesn't it?" He saw Chad's face twitch at the mention of Miles City. Miles City had Letty.

Linus roped the pack animals in file. He led them away and looked back after a hundred yards. Chad and Cully were just turning their horses. Linus wanted to get back to the cabin as quickly as possible. If too much time passed, those two could be at each other's throats.

He knew the value of the pelts, and he did well at the trading post in Fort Benton. The other wolfers usually stayed out all winter. Being first, he received top dollar for his pelts. Fort Benton had no enticements for him, and he didn't tarry. The saddlebags clinked pleasantly as he threw them across his horse's back. He had a little over three hundred dollars in those bags. He intended to divide it evenly—after he took out his share first.

He was within a half hour's ride of the cabin when he dismounted and took a hundred and fifty dollars out of the saddlebags. He buried the money at the foot of the large, distinctive granite block. He would have no trouble in remembering it. He cursed as he hacked away at the frozen ground with his hunting knife.

He squinted at the sky before he remounted. By its heavy, leaden look it was going to snow again. A fresh snow covering would hide all evidence of his digging. He was entitled to a larger share. Wasn't he the brains behind all this?

Chad was standing in the door, when Linus rode up. "You took your time," he said savagely. He was freshly shaved and dressed in clean clothes, and he couldn't hide his eagerness.

Linus didn't argue with him. He shouldered the saddlebags and walked into the cabin. "We did all right," he said heartily.

He counted out the money into three piles. It was in silver dollars, and it made three impressive piles.

"How much?" Chad demanded.

"Fifty-five dollars apiece," Linus said. At Chad's look of disappointment, he asked sharply, "Where can you make better wages anywhere else?"

Chad nodded slow agreement. After all, they had been out less than three weeks. No hired hand could make that kind of money.

He filled his pockets, and the weight of the money was a pleasant thing. He walked to the door. "I don't know when I'll be back."

"Don't stay too long," Linus said. "We're going out again." He grinned as the door closed behind Chad. Chad could only stay as long as his money lasted. And if Linus knew Letty, that wouldn't be very long.

Chad walked into Schober's restaurant, and his eyes were shining. It had been a long time since he had seen her, and a queer breathlessness took him. My God, he groaned silently. She's lovelier than ever. He was glad the place was deserted. He could talk to her without interruption.

A sharpness came into her face as she saw him. "What are you doing here?" She was beginning to believe that after his long absence she was rid of him. But he was back. It wouldn't do him any good.

He stacked silver dollars on the counter without answering her. Each time he added a dollar to the pile, her excitement mounted. Schober paid her poorly, and the room rent took a big bite out of it. It was appalling the way she wore out clothes on this job.

He raised his eyes and said gravely, "Letty?"

It was hard to take her eyes from the stack of dollars. She didn't know how much was there, but it seemed an awfully big pile. These winter nights were cold, and a girl could grow lonely.

"Oh, Chad," she said and leaned over the counter, her arms extended toward him. "You don't know how much I've missed you."

Chad rode despondently back to Linus Derks' cabin. He had spent three nights and two days with Letty. He didn't know time or money could go so fast. But Letty needed so many little things, little things that chewed away at his money until suddenly it was gone. Thinking of those three nights made him feel miserable—not because they were bad. They were just the opposite. They were like the early nights of their marriage. There hadn't been any unwillingness in her, and her flesh had been warm and soft. He supposed he had bragged about making the money, and he had impressed her with rash statements of how he could make all they needed. She believed him. She wanted him to hurry out and make more. She would be waiting for him, just the way she was those three nights.

He groaned with real anguish. He had to be away so many nights to make enough money to be able to spend a pitifully few hours with her. He thought of the exposure, the dirty, monotonous hours, and his misery deepened.

It was beginning to snow as he came in sight of the cabin, and the temperature was dropping. He thought, Linus will probably want to leave in the morning. Rebellion washed through him. He wasn't going with Linus. It wasn't worth it. The memory of three, warm nights overpowered the revolt. He'd go with Linus, if he wanted to spend any more nights with Letty.

Linus looked up as Chad entered the cabin. "I thought you'd be back sooner."

"What do you mean by that?" Chad growled.

Linus grinned. "Nothing." Letty couldn't spend money as fast as he thought she could. He recognized the savage edge to Chad's disposition and honed at it.

He pushed a bottle of whiskey toward him. "It's cold outside. Better warm up your innards."

He watched Chad take a long pull at the bottle. He would let a couple more drinks work on Chad before he sounded him out.

He asked, "You ready to leave in the morning?"

"I guess so," Chad said dispiritedly. He lifted the bottle again. Linus's whiskey was getting better, or he was getting used to the stuff.

"I think we'll go north of the river," Linus said thoughtfully. "Stay out until spring."

Chad's face went startled. Spring was three months away. He slammed his hand down on the table and said violently, "No, by God. I'm not going with you."

"Suit yourself," Linus said pleasantly. "But we're losing too much time coming back here." He watched Chad take another drink. The whiskey should be punching at him. It should make him receptive to new ideas.

He sighed. "I wish there was an easier way to pick up some money. I wish we had some horses to sell."

When Chad set the bottle down for the fourth time, it's level was lowered considerably. The room was getting hot, and the outlines of things were becoming blurred. He had to focus hard to make Linus's face stay in place.

"We haven't got any horses," he growled. "Where would we sell them?"

"I got a friend north of the line. He'll pay a hundred dollars for a good animal." Where McKenzie sold them after Linus delivered them wasn't any of Linus's business. McKenzie didn't ask him any questions. Linus wasn't asking him any.

"We haven't got any horses," Chad repeated stubbornly.

"You know that sorrel you pointed out?" Linus asked. "The one you said you broke. Didn't it make you feel kind of funny seeing it again?"

Chad blinked several times. The damned lamp chimney needed cleaning. "What do you mean?"

"When a man puts that much care and work in on a horse, it seems like it oughta belong to him. McKenzie would pay a hundred dollars for a horse like that."

Chad thought of a hundred dollars. It was a big sum, it was twice the sum he had taken into town with him. He said savagely, "It isn't my horse."

Linus asked, "How much money did Enoch pay you all the years you did a man's work for him?"

"He didn't pay me anything." Enoch bought everything that

was needed. Sometimes he'd put a few dollars in Chad's and Owen's pockets, but he paid no regular salary.

"He didn't pay you?" Linus said in mock astonishment. He shoved the bottle closer to Chad's hand. "Now, that's what I call niggardly. He has to pay his hands thirty dollars a month, doesn't he?"

Chad took the bottle from his mouth. "Something like that, I guess." Was it thirty or forty? He couldn't remember. All his thoughts seemed to have fuzz on them.

"I'd say you been doing a man's work since you were twelve. Six years at three hundred and sixty a year. Do you know what that comes to? Over two thousand dollars. I'd say you earned a few horses."

A spark began to burn through the dull depths of Chad's eyes. All of this was Enoch's fault. He had driven Letty away; he had kept all the money Chad had coming to him.

"Would he miss twenty horses?" Linus asked softly. "Your horses?"

Chad's mind fumbled at figures. Twenty horses. That was two thousand dollars. How many nights was that with Letty? He couldn't figure that far. He only knew it was a lot.

He made a sweep of his arm and knocked over the whiskey bottle. Very little liquid trickled out of it. "They're my horses," he said fiercely. "I've earned every damned one of them."

Linus looked over his head and grinned at Cully. "You're going to need some help, Chad. And we're going to give you all the help you need."

EIGHTEEN

After the first storm, Enoch kept saying, "We'll have an early winter and get it over with." Owen didn't bother to answer him. He doubted Enoch believed his own words. If he did, he wasted a lot of tense scrutiny on the sky.

Owen did expect a chinook after the first storm, or at least, a partial warm-up. It didn't come. The temperature hovered well below freezing, and the snow cover stayed on the ground. It was frightening to see how deeply they were cutting into the hay, and November wasn't over yet. The days were raw and cold. When a man came in at night, his hands and feet hurt. Owen learned to live with the constant ache in his jaw. It wouldn't be so bad, if you felt like you were accomplishing something. He and Enoch had talked about the haystacks and decided they couldn't open them to the hungry cattle. They couldn't satisfy the hunger of the animals. The best they could do was to keep them alive. It took time to fork loose hay onto a wagon and haul it out. It had to be forked onto the ground, and each forkful disappeared almost before it landed. At the day's end, the cattle still bawled as hungrily as they did in the morning, and a man was savage with frustration.

THE LONG COLD WIND

The Texas cattle were in a weakened condition, when the first storm hit, and as near as Owen could tally, they had lost close to a hundred head. Daily, he added an additional head or two to the mounting loss. Those cows had been too weak to go into winter; they became more feeble and laid down and died. When a cow made up her mind to die, she just laid down and never got up again.

December brought two more blizzards, the last one intense. There was little or no conversation in the house any more. Enoch sat and stared blankly, and Owen saw a visible aging in him. Molly tried to ease the strain, but even she gave up against the wall of Enoch's brooding. All they could do was sit and wait for better weather. The waiting and the helplessness were crushing weights on a man's soul.

The Indians called January the Moon of Cold-Exploding Trees. Freezing sap expanded, bursting trees into shreds, and the reports sounded like cannon shot. On the ninth of January it started snowing. It snowed without a minute's letup for sixteen hours, and it averaged an inch an hour. The temperature dropped to twenty-two degrees below zero, and the world turned white, a cruel, frozen white. The wind screamed in laughter at the puny efforts man made to save himself and his stock. He could dole out wisps of hay, when mountainous piles were needed, he could try to dig cattle out of drifts and break up the bunching near the fences. Three or four men could work a half day digging a single cow out of a drift, then see her take a few steps and collapse and die. Men cursed the weather and the country. They cursed God for letting it happen.

It snowed intermittently for another ten days, and the temperature knew only one way to go—down. The flesh seemed to waste from Enoch's face, and his skin hung in loose, leathery folds. Owen thought, why, he's old. He had often referred to Enoch as the old man, but it was a title, not a description. Now it was a description.

But a stubborn, savage spark remained in Enoch's eyes. He drove himself relentlessly, and he drove the others even harder. No matter what a man accomplished it was never enough. He wanted a man in the saddle before morning's light and until after dark. He wanted report after report of how the cattle were doing. He was like a man embarked on wild, senseless self-destruction, and each report killed a bit of him. But he had to know. The men were driven to the point of open rebellion. The only thing that stopped it was that Enoch drove himself just as hard.

Owen came into the kitchen after dark. He was so tired he staggered, and he ached from the cold. For a few moments, the heat in the room was cruel, stirring his numbed circulation into life and burning like hot wires.

Enoch looked at him. His eyes were the only things that seemed alive in him these days. "What's it doing outside?" It was the one, constant question. He asked it morning and night.

"Getting colder." Owen drew off his gloves and stood before the stove, rubbing life back into his hands. "Clouds piling up. Looks like we're in for another one."

He saw the wild, agonized protest in Enoch's eyes, then the eyes turned dull and Enoch's head drooped.

This is breaking him, Owen thought, and he wasn't referring to material loss. He felt a pity for Enoch, the first he had known in years.

He saw the worry in Molly's eyes and shook his head. Nobody could do anything. There were no words, no effort that was any good. There was only the helpless waiting, and that crushed a man's spirit.

Enoch toyed with his evening meal. Molly scolded him for not eating, and if he heard her, he gave no sign. Enoch was listening to a stronger voice, the voice of the increasing wind.

Owen said, "We're missing some horses."

Enoch grunted. He wasn't worried about the horses. Not when worry for the cattle filled his head.

"We are," Owen insisted. "Remember that sorrel Chad broke?" He glanced at Molly and saw the twinge of pain in her face. He couldn't recall the name. "The sorrel's gone and maybe a half-dozen others."

"They drifted," Enoch said listlessly.

"The others didn't drift. We've got to get a count tomorrow."

Enoch's face remained blank, and Owen thought wearily, all right. I'll do it myself. Those horses are gone. I know it.

He pushed aside his unfinished meal and walked to the door. The wind was getting stronger. He did not have to open the door to know the temperature was dropping. He could feel the cold stealing through the cracks around the door. Tonight, the white frost line on the floor would creep over nearer the stove.

He put on his mackinaw and gloves and looked at Molly. "I'd better bring in more wood."

Enoch's eyes remained vacant. Owen thought angrily, he might offer to help. The thrust of anger disappeared. Enoch was digging himself deep into his own thoughts. A man could dig too deep that way, and sometimes, he couldn't get back.

He shook his head and opened the door. The wind buffeted him, and he could feel particles of stinging cold against his face. It was snowing again. He thought wearily, it can't last much longer. There're only four days left in January.

The worst blizzard of the season struck during the night. The house rocked under the wind, and outside was a howling, white wilderness. The frost line on the floor crept to within three feet of the stove, and the stove had to be red-hot to keep it back that far. Molly and Enoch and Owen spent the early hours of the morning huddled around the stove. The cold in the bedrooms and the howling wind made sleep impossible.

Enoch muttered, "As soon as it gets light, we'll have to see to the cattle."

They wouldn't see to the cattle this morning, Owen thought grimly. They wouldn't move from shelter until this storm blew itself out.

It lasted for three days. Even in the middle of the day it was impossible to see more than fifty feet in any direction. Snow didn't fall. It rode the wild wind on horizontal planes, and the drifts grew mountainous. Owen didn't believe the thermometer outside the kitchen. It registered sixty degrees below zero. Mere survival took tremendous effort. The woodpile shrank, and Owen was afraid it wouldn't last until he could cut more. Keeping a path open from house to outbuildings was a Herculean task. As fast as a man shoveled away the relentless white weight, more of it fell. At first, a man knew wild rage, and he worked the harder for it. Then a weakening sense of futility crept in, sapping the strength from his muscles. It was hard to keep from quitting, hard to keep the spark of resistance alive.

At the end of three days, the wind shifted and the temperature rose. It didn't rise a great deal, but it was an improvement. And men rode out to see how bad it was, to save what was left.

Owen put on two suits of heavy underwear and two pairs of wool socks. He stuffed the tails of two woolen shirts into woolen pants. He pulled on overalls, then his chaps. His hands were awkward with the wool gloves under leather mittens, and the blanket-lined overcoat further burdened him. He looked twice his size, and he moved awkwardly. He found the first day that even all these clothes weren't enough. The cold numbed his feet first, then crept up his legs.

An hour's work exhausted man and animal. Horses breasted deep snow, and a rider who dismounted stepped into snow waist-deep on the level.

What cattle they found were half dead from cold and hunger. There was little that could be done for them. If shelter were fairly close, they tried to herd the cattle toward it. They dug them out of drifts, only to see them stagger into another one a dozen steps farther on. It made Owen physically ill to look at the poor, shambling beasts. Their bodies were covered with sores and frozen blood, and they moved as though they were blind. Men expended tremendous effort, but they couldn't accomplish much. They could keep the bewildered, freezing cattle away from the treacherous air holes in the rivers, they could dig a few out of drifts. Owen thought bitterly, it might have been kinder to let the cattle slip into the air holes and get it over with.

A man learned little tricks that made survival not easy but easier. He could keep his feet warmer by walking in snow in his bare feet, then rubbing them dry before he put on his socks. After pulling on his boots, he would stand in water, then move outdoors until an airtight sheath of ice formed over the boots. The coating would last for hours and was windproof. He blacked his face and eye sockets with lampblack or burnt matches as protection against snow blindness, or cut holes in a black neckerchief that masked his face. But whatever he did was never quite enough. He still froze hands and feet, and icy air stabbed into lungs and stomach. Worst of all, he could not keep the cattle from dying. The animals froze to death where they stood in drifts, they blundered against fences and piled up and died. Or they ventured out on the treacherously thin ice around the air holes in the river and disappeared. Each day new losses added to the staggering enormity of the losses already behind them. A man's mind refused to grasp just how bad the losses were. He really wouldn't know until spring. The wind drifted snow over many of the carcasses, hiding them, and maybe it was a relief to minds already overburdened.

THE LONG COLD WIND

Owen's horse trembled with fatigue as he turned its head toward home. Scotty was behind him, and they had cut time for the return trip thin. They would be lucky to reach the buildings before darkness caught them. They rode single file, keeping to the path they had beaten down in riding this far. Owen doubted either horse had endurance left to break new trail. He knew he would be glad to see Scotty inside. Scotty looked bad this morning, and Owen had suggested he remain behind. Scotty had been almost angry in his refusal. But that racking cough should have been given some attention, and Owen didn't like the grayness in Scotty's face. He thought with partial anger, a man has his foolish pride. Scotty wouldn't stay in and take care of himself, while the others went on.

They rode silently, each man wrapped about in his individual, gloomy thoughts. It was going to be cold tonight, but it would be a still cold. That alone would be a relief after the successive days of wind.

Owen raised his voice. "Scotty, maybe this is the last big storm of the winter." It had to end sometime, and the chinook usually came in February. It'll come too late to save a lot of us, he thought. Nobody would be trailing big herds in here next summer. He had been right on every point, and he wished he had been wrong.

He hadn't heard Scotty's cough for several steps, and he said, "Scotty?" He slewed about in his saddle to look behind him.

Scotty's horse stood riderless some thirty yards behind Owen. Owen knew a quick, hurting constriction in his throat. He turned and made his way back. He threw off and plowed snow to where Scotty lay. Scotty lay face down, almost buried in snow, and Owen was sure he was dead. He turned him over and saw the feebling flaring and closing of the nostrils.

He said roughly, "Come on, Scotty. We're almost home. Hang on."

Scotty opened his eyes and tried to smile. "I didn't make it to spring," he said, and died.

Owen came into the kitchen with dragging steps. Molly took one look at him and knew something was wrong. She said quietly, "I was worried about you. What happened?"

Enoch turned his head to listen.

The tears were scalding hot inside Owen, but they couldn't

force themselves into his eyes. His eyes were hot and prickly, and they needed the washing of tears. He said, "Scotty died out there in the snow. I think he was just too tired to go on."

Molly's face twisted, and she said, "No."

Enoch stared blankly as though he didn't understand.

"Didn't you hear me?" Owen shouted. "He died out there in the snow trying to save the cattle you kept forcing on the range."

Enoch seemed to collapse inwardly, and what remained was a thin, shrunken shell. He stared at the table top, and Owen wondered what he actually saw. Did he see the loyalty, the years of friendship from Scotty. He wanted to hammer those things at Enoch. He wanted him to suffer as cruelly as Scotty had suffered.

Molly put her hand on his coat sleeve. She said, "No, Owen," and it brought him back to sanity. She was right. He could accuse Enoch until his voice was hoarse, and it wouldn't change a thing.

His face was wooden as he took off his outer garments. He rubbed his jaw and didn't realize he was doing it.

Molly asked in a faltering voice, "You didn't leave him out there?"

He said harshly, "I brought him back." Scotty's body was frozen stiff by the time Owen had reached the barn. He had had trouble in untying and lowering him to the ground.

Molly said, "I'll go to him."

"No." He didn't mean his voice to sound so curt, but she could do nothing for Scotty. Scotty would be all right where he was—until spring. In a way, Scotty would see his spring, for the ground was too frozen to dig a grave. Scotty's burial had to wait until after the first thaw.

Molly asked bewilderedly, "But where is he?"

Owen turned on her. She kept asking questions, she had to know. He said savagely, "I put him in a snowbank behind the barn. He'll stay there until spring."

NINETEEN

The prick of his conscience was a thorn in Chad's heel. Every now and then, he forgot and came down on it hard, and he felt its sharp, painful thrust. The trick was to give it no weight by not thinking about it. That was hard to do. He could put a big whiskey lake in his mind, and thoughts could still swim through it.

He scowled and pulled at a knuckle. He should have no complaints. Everything had gone just as Linus said it would. He had over a hundred dollars in his pockets, and Letty would be waiting for him. It hadn't taken any time at all. Three days from start to finish saw the job done. They had taken six horses, and the storm covered their tracks. Linus was clever in judging the coming of a storm. He could call them almost to the hour.

He did have one complaint, he thought fiercely. Linus had no right to bring in those other two men. Benton's son was a year younger than Chad, and Chad didn't like him. Sugg Benton had narrow, shifty eyes, and he talked too much. He kept saying, "Pa's afraid of these big ranchers. By God, I'm not."

Chad thought, if he says it once more, I'm going to paste him. He didn't care much more for Dougan's brother, Ord. Ord was a fat man with a weak mouth. He had an annoying habit of rubbing his hands together. Ord was scared of those big ranchers. Chad grinned as he remembered how Ord had tried to drive those horses by looking behind him all the time.

Maybe Linus was right. Maybe they did need the extra help. But he could've picked better men, Chad thought gloomily. His face brightened as he saw the lights of Miles City ahead of him. He was going to beat the storm into town. There seemed to be a lot of cattle piling up around town, and he wondered who had driven them here. Surely no one could be considering shipping in this kind of weather. His face was sober as he thought of cattle. Spring was going to uncover tremendous losses for the ranchers. He had seen many dead cattle. He swore softly and pushed the thoughts out of his head. It was none of his concern now. He was out of that phase of it.

He touched spurs to his mount. For the next week he wouldn't be thinking of cold or snow or cattle. He would be thinking about nothing but Letty.

The going wasn't bad by the time Owen reached the outskirts of Miles City. The milling cattle had trampled down the snow. He thought, surely no one's trying to drive in this kind of weather. They couldn't make two miles a day, and if another storm hit them out on the trail, the whole herd would be lost.

It had been a hard trip to town, and only the need of supplies forced him to make it. Now his progress was slowed to a crawl by the cattle in Miles City's streets. Kilmonte will raise hell, he thought, if somebody doesn't get these cattle out of here.

He kept yelling at them to clear a passage for his horse, and the cattle shuffled slowly to one side. He had looked at too many cattle like these in the past weeks. These animals were nothing but racks of bones, covered by scuffy hides. They bawled incessantly, and they staggered as they moved. Something suddenly hit him. He was looking at a dozen different brands. This was no herd, gathered for a drive. These were individual animals, forgetting their instinctive distrust of man and pulled toward town in their last hope of finding food and shelter. He saw McLaughlin's cattle and Denton's. There were even a few head of E-P cattle. Up ahead of him, an old roan cow coughed and sank slowly to her knees. She made a brief struggle to get back on her hoofs, then sagged on her side. Main Street would be partially blocked until she was dragged away.

Owen stopped before Kilmonte's office and walked inside.

Kilmonte was standing with his back toward the stove, and unreasonably, Owen felt a sweeping rage. It was a big rage; it included all the people in town. Men died trying to save their cattle, while the townspeople toasted their asses at their stoves.

Kilmonte put a brooding glance on him.

Owen said, "You've got a dead cow on Main Street."

Kilmonte swore fluently. He ran down and said, "You cattlemen are going to have to keep your cattle out of town."

"How?" Owen challenged.

Kilmonte's shoulders drooped. "There isn't any way, I guess. I doubt if there's a fence left uncut in the whole country."

Owen nodded. He had cut every one he found to prevent the cattle from piling up against it. He guessed other ranchers had been doing the same. A man could sink in his own fight and forget that other people had the same kind of a fight.

Kilmonte's face was gloomy. "I'm sick of seeing these animals die right out in front of my office."

Owen blew out a breath. "You're sick! You should own those animals, you should see them die by the fifties and hundreds."

"They've eaten things I thought cattle wouldn't touch," Kilmonte said. "They've eaten all the garbage in town. They've chewed down the bushes and trees people have planted. I got a complaint this morning from Mrs. Watkins. Her two lilac bushes, she had sent all the way from St. Louis, were eaten down to the ground. She wanted to know what I was going to do about it."

He didn't look at Owen as he asked, "Are you going to save anything?"

Owen shook his head. He didn't know. The rage was still with him. He didn't want sympathy from Kilmonte. He said, "We're losing horses."

Kilmonte grunted. The grunt said, are you surprised? With this kind of weather.

"Not the weather," Owen said angrily. "Somebody's running them off. We're shy a dozen head. I think somebody's letting the storms cover their tracks."

"What do you want me to do about it?" Kilmonte asked flatly.

Owen stared at him, then he shouted, "I want you to find out who it is. I want it stopped."

Kilmonte stared at him. "You can't track them, or you would have done it without coming here. Do you know who's behind it, or where they're driving them, or who they're selling to?" He shook his head, covering all the answers. "You expect me to just ride around out there until I stumble across them?"

Owen said hotly, "I don't expect you to do anything." He stalked to the door and stopped. "You'll keep pretty busy dragging cows off Main Street."

Kilmonte shouted at him, "You give me something to go on. You walk in here with nothing but suspicions—"

Owen shut the door on the rest of Kilmonte's words. He walked toward Hillsdale's saloon. He tried to force his anger to drown out the face of his unreasonableness. He couldn't even say positively the horses were stolen. He just had that uneasiness, and the horses were gone. He admitted they could have drifted to some other part of the range, or that wolves had pulled them down, or that they had died and would be covered until spring. He hadn't been very fair with Kilmonte. The admission only increased his anger.

He stepped inside the saloon and McLaughlin and Denton were seated at a table. Both of them were owl-eyed drunk.

Denton waved an expansive hand. "Sit down, Owen. Join us, while we watch everything we have swept away."

Owen pulled out a chair. He wanted to ask about Evlalie. The scar tissue wasn't very thick. Just the thought of her opened up the old wound.

He didn't blame them for getting drunk. At times, a man didn't seem to have any other resource. Tomorrow, they would be trying as hard as ever, but tonight, they were trying to forget it.

McLaughlin said, "I'm through trying to save dying cows. It's no use, anyhow."

Denton nodded heavy approval. "Let 'em all die. Every damned one of them."

Addie should hear him now, Owen thought, and his lips quirked. She'd take a broom and knock the nonsense out of him in a hurry.

He poured himself a drink and asked, "Are we going to have anything left?"

McLaughlin's face twisted with raw passion. "Not a damned thing. It'll stay cold past the Fourth of July. There won't be a cow left on the range."

Denton nodded solemn agreement and reached for the

bottle. McLaughlin took it out of his hand and filled Denton's glass for him.

If Owen was going to get sensible talk out of these two, he'd better be at it. "Are either of you missing any horses?"

"Missing everything," Denton said.

"Tom." Owen's sharp tone pulled up Denton's head. "Who in hell could tell?" he asked sullenly. "With this weather."

McLaughlin was trying to keep his eyes fixed on Owen's face. He treated the question seriously, and he wanted to give an equally sober answer. "A couple of times, I thought I was. But I never got an accurate count. I just figured they'd drifted."

"Just a few of them drifted?" Owen asked. "And the rest stayed on familiar range?"

McLaughlin blinked several times. "You missing horses, Owen?" he asked softly.

"I know I am."

Denton focused his eyes on Owen. "It might be a good season for somebody to operate, Owen. With all these storms to cover their tracks. You got any ideas?"

"None," Owen said curtly. "I talked to Kilmonte about it. He won't move unless I can bring him proof."

McLaughlin and Denton spent several moments cursing Kilmonte and his office. Denton said thickly, "If we had proof, we wouldn't have to ask Kilmonte's help. He leaned across the table and peered at Owen. "You think Derks is in it?"

"Not this time," Owen said shortly. He didn't tell them his reason. He had heard Chad was living with Derks. Chad would never stand for horses being stolen off E-P land. If Derks were doing it, Chad would certainly know about it.

He stood and poured himself another drink. He tossed it down and set the empty glass on the table. The whiskey warmth would help on the cold ride home.

He said, "Keep your eyes open. We're hurt enough without someone stripping our horses from us."

Both of them gave him sober nods. "The first sign you get let us know," McLaughlin said.

Owen grinned at him. "One of your cows dropped dead on the street. Kilmonte wants you to drag it away."

He chuckled mirthlessly as McLaughlin made a ribald suggestion as to what Kilmonte could do with the cow. He looked back at the door, and they were pouring another round.

Their original determination to get drunk hadn't weakened. Neither would their statement about help, when he found the horse thieves, weaken. They would file that away in their minds. It would be there when they sobered up in the morning.

He stepped on the walk, instinctively glancing at the sky. He did it every time he walked outdoors, always praying to see a clear sky. The sky was cloudy. The air was heavy and holding. It had the feeling of more snow in it.

It looked as if February was going the same way as December and January. Half of it was gone, and a man was even afraid to think snow and cold for fear the weather would act in accordance with his thoughts. Owen only knew it snowed too damned easy. The hay was all gone. There was nothing more anyone could do for the cattle. A few of the hardiest might stagger through to spring, but the losses would be staggering.

He groaned as he looked at the leaden sky. Not another storm, he thought. It had been threatening for the past two days, and this afternoon it looked as though the threat was coming to a head.

Why didn't a man give up? Why didn't he gather what he could carry with him and ride south, out of this hell of cold and suffering? A man thought about it, but he never did anything about it. Maybe the Creator knew what He was doing, when He put that stubborn spark in a man, making him struggle on long after struggle was practical.

He sighed and turned his horse toward home. He hesitated a moment, then decided to cut the angle instead of going the longer way around. It would save considerable distance. Against that saved distance was the fact of rougher ground, with the snow making travel rough. It still lay deep on the ground, though it had settled from its earlier depth. Would the time saved by the shorter distance be lost by bucking unbroken snow? He decided to save the distance.

He hadn't gone a half mile, when he saw the trampled-down lane in the snow. He stared at it a long moment without fully comprehending what it was. A hard, savage excitement began to throb in his veins. He was looking at the trail of horses, of how many horses he couldn't say, for hoofprint was piled on top of hoofprint. He could be looking at the trail of a dozen horses and even more. Those horses hadn't been drifting aimlessly, for this trampled path ran straight. Some human agency was forcing those horses along on a straight course.

He squinted toward the north. The river lay that way. Maybe the thieves' luck had run out. The storm, by holding off, had left their tracks bare.

He debated a brief moment, then reined his mount toward the north. He couldn't take the time to go home and get help. If it started snowing, an hour's fall could blot out those tracks.

He stirred his horse to a faster pace. Kilmonte thought he was crazy, did he? Maybe Kilmonte would eat his words.

He gave his horse a breather after a couple of hours' ride. He judged he was some fifteen miles below the mouth of the Musselshell, though it was hard for him to establish accurately just where he was. If he remembered right, there was an old abandoned woodyard on the river. When steamboat traffic was heavy, the woodyard had been active, though for the past few years, it had been deserted. He tried to get a mental picture of its location. There should be a log cabin there with a log corral attaching cabin and stable. It was a lonely site; it would be particularly bleak in this kind of weather. It could be an ideal stopping place for men whose next jump was across the river into Canada.

He dismounted and proceeded on foot, covering the next few hundred yards with infinite care. If his memory wasn't faulty, he would look down on the woodyard from a height of ground. The height was covered with trees and brush, affording him some protection against being seen. He was going to feel pretty empty, if that old woodyard was still abandoned.

He crawled to the edge of the height, and the woodyard and its buildings were spread out before him. He lay there a long time, ignoring the cold stealing into his body. Anger burned inside him, anger enough to offset the cold. He could see no people, but there was smoke curling from the chimney of the cabin. And in the corral, ten or twelve horses milled about.

He backed carefully away. He didn't know who the people in that cabin were, but the proof he needed was in that corral. He had been too far away to make out brands, but he knew some of the horses in that corral carried E-P. Kilmonte would act on what Owen saw, but he wasn't going to get the chance. Owen would get help; he needed help, but he and Enoch, McLaughlin and Denton, and perhaps a few others would handle this.

He had a momentary fear the men and horses would be gone by the time he returned. He looked up as snow touched his face. It drove the fear away. Men wouldn't leave the shelter of the cabin in a storm. They would wait it out, secure in the false belief no one knew anything about them.

It was snowing pretty hard by the time he reached his horse. It would be almost dark by the time he got home. It was going to be a wet, cold ride, but for the first time in weeks, his mind wasn't filled with the weather.

TWENTY

A half circle of tired, cold, angry men was drawn about the woodyard. The river kept them from surrounding the cabin completely. It had taken time to gather this many men, and they had ridden through the night to reach this place. McLaughlin had brought three men with him, Denton had two. Owen and Enoch, Les, Hamp and Abel were on the upper end of the line. They used the waning moments of darkness to creep closer to the cabin, and each yard closed the line tighter. The horses in the corral knew something was out there. Owen could hear their nervous snorting and the stamp of their hoofs. With the strengthening light he could see their forms between the corral bars. He stared intently, then said in a flat voice, "I know that roan."

Enoch nodded. He had come alive. His eyes burned, and a flush of color was in his face. He had an abiding hatred for horse thieves, and the promise of the coming moment strengthened him.

He said grudgingly, "You were right. We'll end it here." It was as close as he could come to outright praise.

Down the line a man coughed, and Enoch scowled at him. He put his eyes back on the cabin. He lay in the fresh snow, impervious to its creeping cold. He could wait as long as necessary without a thought of physical discomfort.

Owen watched the silent cabin. He didn't know how many men were inside it, but it would take only a few to make a fort of it. And attackers, going against those walls, could suffer heavy losses. He wanted to prevent that, and surprise could be his ally.

He said, "If some of us can get to the door before they know we're here, we might take them without firing a shot."

Enoch said savagely, "I don't want them shot. I want them alive."

Owen looked at him strangely and said, "Cover me." He moved forward fifteen yards and crouched behind the brush. He waited, his muscles tense, and heard no outcry showing he was discovered. The horses knew he was there. Their restlessness increased. Owen wondered why the men in the cabin didn't come out to investigate. They had to be sodden drunk or asleep or gone. He knew a quick dismay at the last supposition. If the cabin were empty, it would be a sickening disappointment. Those men could have left last night, leaving the horses behind them. The horses would be regained, but it wouldn't stop further stealing.

He waited thirty seconds, and no life showed from the cabin. He waved his arm, and Les joined him, covering the distance with a short burst of speed, then diving to the ground and breaking his fall with the butt of his rifle.

Owen frowned at him. Les should have crawled. The eye picked up rapid movement quicker than anything else. He let the seconds drag away and saw no stir of life from the cabin.

He signaled again, this time indicating caution, and Denton crawled to them. He didn't want Denton, he wanted one of the others. He was thinking of Evlalie and Addie. At any moment, those cabin walls could be ablaze with rifle and pistol fire.

Denton saw the protest in Owen's face and said in a low voice, "Save your breath. I'm not going back."

McLaughlin was the last man to join them. The others would stay back, covering the cabin. At the first shot from it, they would blast those walls, forcing the defenders to stay down.

The four moved, a man at a time, leapfrogging the intervening distance to the cabin. Owen felt more naked with every yard he advanced, and his skin was tight in fearful anticipation of a bullet. A short jump would carry him to the corral walls, and he would not draw an easy breath until he was pressed against those logs. He made it and touched his forehead. As cold as it was he was sweating.

From here he had another angle of fire at the cabin door, a cross fire. If a man stepped out that door, he would be riddled from two sources, by his rifle, and from the rifles behind him.

He watched the door until McLaughlin, Denton, and Les joined him. Their faces showed the same strain he had known. That last stretch tightened a man's guts and made his breathing hurt.

Denton whispered, "I expected a bullet to plow into me any second."

McLaughlin nodded grave agreement. He used the same low tone. "Is anybody in there, Owen?"

"We'll see," Owen said. At least, the horse thieves had been here. He hadn't cost these men a long, hard trip for nothing.

It was relatively simple to move from the corral, across the front of the cabin and take their places, two on each side of the door. The horses, in the corral, were going wild, their frightened neighing a blast of sound. If anyone was in that cabin they couldn't overlook that commotion.

Owen stiffened as he heard the voice. The cabin walls muffled it, and the speaker must be yelling for Owen to hear him. "Ord," the voice said. "Go see what's the matter with those horses."

Owen looked at the hard, bright shine in the eyes of McLaughlin and Les, across the door from him. This was their answer. He made a gesture of caution, wanting no impatient move to spoil it now. The door was going to be opened for them.

The door opened, and a man appeared framed in it. His mouth was open in a yawn, and his eyes were still sleepy. Some instinct warned him, and he half turned his head. His eyes went wide at the sight of Owen, and his mouth opened wider for the yell that never came.

Owen slammed the rifle butt into that opened mouth. He hoped to knock the man back into the cabin, but it didn't go that way. Ord's legs went limber as string, and he fell into Owen. Behind him, McLaughlin, Denton, and Les pushed hard against him in their eagerness to get inside, and there was a jam in the doorway.

Owen fought Ord's sagging bulk. Ord fell and pulled him with him. He had a confused impression of the interior of the cabin as he fell. He couldn't say how many men were in it. Four, maybe five, and each showed varying degrees of surprise. One was squatted down by the stove, holding a stick of firewood, and Owen thought two were near the rear of the cabin. As he fell, the man at the stove hurled the stick of firewood at Owen, and it crashed into the wall near his head. McLaughlin, Denton, and Les trampled him in their wild eagerness to get inside. Someone in the cabin recovered quickly, for Owen heard the report of a pistol.

McLaughlin grunted and sat down suddenly as if something had kicked his legs out from under him. Les fell over him. He fired as he was going down, and someone in the cabin uttered a shrill scream.

Ord's limp weight was still across Owen, and he fought to throw it off. There was no real resistance in the man, but his fingers kept clawing feebly at Owen.

He cursed as he heaved at the weight and threw it from him. He had Les and McLaughlin to scramble around, and when he jumped to his feet, the rear door was open.

Denton's pistol was pointed at Cully Derks. Cully's hands were high in the air, and his face showed a sullen impassiveness.

"One move," Denton said, "and I'll blow your head off."

Les got to his feet and bent over the man he had shot. "It's Sugg Benton," he said.

"Dead?" Owen asked.

Les shook his head. "Shoulder's shattered." He listened indifferently to Sugg's groaning.

McLaughlin sat on the floor, staring at his leg. A spreading patch of crimson showed on his pants leg just above the knee.

Owen asked, "Is it bad?"

McLaughlin grunted, "I don't know. I don't feel anything yet." He looked at Owen, wonder in his eyes. "It was just like somebody kicked my leg out from under me."

McLaughlin would feel pain later on. At the moment, shock was a merciful wall, keeping the pain away.

"How many went out the back door?" Owen asked Denton.

"One, I think." Denton scowled. "Everything happened so fast, I'm not sure. I didn't hear any shots from outside. The others should have seen him."

Maybe not, Owen thought. The cabin would have shielded the man until he reached the riverbank. Once he reached that protective bank, he would be hard to see.

"Who was it, Cully?" Owen asked.

Cully spat at him.

Denton made a threatening gesture toward him, and Owen said, "It doesn't matter. Whoever it was can't get far on foot."

He walked to the rear door. "Watch them," he said and stepped outside. Except for the man who had escaped, he had a surprisingly easy victory.

He saw the path plowed to the river's edge. The snow was calf deep, and the great, plunging strides showed how the man had fought it. The tracks didn't show more than one man.

Owen followed the trail, stepping in the deep tracks. It was easier going than breaking fresh trail. He expected to pin his man at the river. He's armed, he thought. And the surprise is gone. He won't give up without a fight.

It came as no surprise that Cully had been in the cabin. Hadn't Enoch always said the Derkses were horse thieves? Linus must have been the one who escaped. At the first sign of trouble he had slipped out the rear door. Owen grunted. It fit Linus Derks. Enoch's eyes would gleam, when Owen brought him back.

Even with the snow, he momentarily lost the tracks at the river's edge. Linus was traveling fast. Owen hadn't caught sight of him. He stood at the river's edge, debating his course. Its edge was brushy, and jumbled boulders ran down to the river. It was encased in silent ice, and the wind had broomed its wide expanse free of snow. Owen frowned. Linus could cross on the ice all right, but he hadn't been that far ahead. If he were out on the river, Owen would be able to see the moving figure.

He stared at the ice, and his face cleared. Derks must have taken a wide half circle on the ice to break his tracks, then cut back to the bank. Somewhere along this bank, Owen would pick up his tracks again. But which way did he go—up or down.

Behind him, he heard faint shouts. He wished he had waited for help, then both directions could be covered at once. He couldn't afford to wait now, or to go back for help. He couldn't give Derks that much time.

He made his decision and turned up the riverbank. He went less than two hundred yards and found where Derks had left the ice. He found a bleak pleasure at the sight of the tracks.

He followed the tracks for a quarter of a mile, then they

disappeared again at the ice's edge. Owen kept moving up the river. Derks was making another half circle on the ice to break his tracks again.

It was rough going here, and the bank rose high above the ice's edge. Owen swore at the brush and slippery rocks. He covered five hundred yards, and the snow was unbroken. He stopped in perplexity. He decided it was useless going farther. Derks hadn't had that much time. Somewhere he had missed those tracks coming off the ice. Or Derks had crossed the river. Owen's scowl grew. He couldn't believe that. He had kept an eye on the river as he moved along it.

He retraced his steps and stopped where the bank was highest. The elevation gave him an unobstructed view in all directions. The expanse of snow was unbroken, and he saw no moving dot on the ice.

He cursed in an outrage of spirit. The man he wanted most had gotten away. The only thing he could do now was to return to the cabin and get more men for a thorough search. It would take time, and every minute Derks was getting farther away.

He started on the return journey, and he got the queer feeling someone was near him. He looked in all directions, and saw nothing. Still, the odd feeling persisted. He looked at the edge of the ice below him. A small amount of snow, no bigger than a handful, was lodged in the roughened surface of the ice. It wasn't big enough to take an entire footprint, but it looked freshly flattened as though someone had stepped on it.

Some of these tall banks were undercut by the restless motion of the water. He had seen undercuts as big as a cave. This bank could be hollowed out. The man he wanted could be crouched right under his feet.

He said quietly, "Come out of there."

He thought for a moment he must be fooling himself, then from the bank's edge, a man's head rose into view. The sickness in him grew at the sight of the familiar face. He said brokenly, "You."

"You looking for someone else, Owen?" Chad asked. He pulled himself up onto the bank and dropped the pistol he held. His grin was bleak. "I could've shot you in the back."

Owen stared at his brother, and his thoughts were a whirling torment. He said savagely, "You threw in with them?"

Chad shrugged. "It was a living." He seemed tired and uncaring.

"Linus got out with you. Where is he?"

Mockery was behind Chad's eyes. "Linus? Why, I haven't seen him for weeks."

He was lying, and Owen knew it. While he was tracking Chad, Linus had gotten away. Why couldn't it have been the other way around?

Chad said, "You can turn me loose, or take me back. Which way is it going to be?"

Owen struggled with his decision. Chad was a horse thief. He had no more rights than the others in the cabin. But Chad was his brother. It wasn't fair that Linus got away, while Owen had to take Chad back.

Chad asked mockingly, "You having trouble deciding?"

Before Owen could answer, Enoch's voice bellowed. "Owen. Who you got there? Did you find another one of them?"

Owen turned his head. Four men were making their way toward him, and Enoch was in the lead.

Chad said, "You took too long, Owen."

Owen saw the shock seize the four men's faces as they saw who he had. Hamp's and Abel's jaws worked in an agony of embarrassment, and Denton looked at the ground, his hands playing with his rifle stock.

Enoch said, "You." It was the only word he uttered to Chad. His face was rock-hard as he stared at him, and some wild savagery worked in his eyes. He seemed to shrivel. He seemed to melt into smaller dimensions, and Owen guessed it was because the way his shoulders sagged and his back bent.

Enoch said, "Bring him along," and turned back to the cabin.

Some kind of relief flickered in Cully's eyes, when he saw who the prisoner was. Or at least, Owen took it for relief. Two men had gotten out of the cabin. Linus Derks was the other—and he was free.

The four prisoners stood against an outside wall of the cabin. Ord Dougan sniffled softly with the pain of his aching jaw, and Sugg Benton clutched his wounded shoulder. Cully stared straight at Enoch and Owen, the hating undiminished in his eyes. Chad looked at Owen, and Owen thought a ghost of a grin played at his lip corners.

Enoch said tersely, "Hang them."

For a moment, the order froze Owen, then he sprang forward and said hoarsely, "No."

Enoch fixed him with a piercing gaze. "Isn't that what horse thieves usually get? What do you say we do with them?"

Everyone stared at Owen, and he fumbled with his words. "I thought we'd take them to Kilmonte."

Enoch shook his head, and there was finality in the gesture. "I said hang them."

Owen stepped in front of him. "You won't." Enoch didn't realize what he was saying. Chad was among those four. "That's Chad," he cried. "That's your son."

Enoch's face looked like a death mask. "Not my son," he said. "A horse thief."

Before Owen could guess at Enoch's intent, Enoch raised the rifle he was holding. He brought the barrel down in a brutal stroke, and Owen tried to duck. He was too late. The barrel clipped him across the forehead, and the blackness was quick and complete.

He came to in a throbbing sea of pain. His head was a cork, bobbing on that sea. For a moment, the pain was a barrier, blocking any coherent thought. Then he remembered, and he tried to sit up. The sudden movement threatened to tear off the top of his head, and his teeth clenched back a yell.

He made it and sat there, holding his head, until the nausea subsided. He looked up and Les and Hamp and Abel were grouped about him. Their faces were rigid with strain, and their eyes would not quite meet his.

Hamp asked, "You feel like riding, Owen?"

Owen did not need anything else to tell him it was all over. There was numbed incredulity in those eyes that looked at him as if they could not yet understand what had happened.

He knocked aside proffered hands of help and stood on shaky legs. Denton was helping McLaughlin to his saddle. McLaughlin swore through clenched teeth at the hurting in his wounded leg.

Off to one side, Enoch was lashing a blanket-covered body to a horse. No one spoke to him, or offered help. He had built a wall around him as tangible as though it were constructed of granite.

Owen strode to him. "He's no different than the others. Why didn't you leave him here with them?"

Enoch's face was remote, but his hands were steady. He didn't even glance at Owen.

Owen's feeling rose in an overpowering wave. He didn't attempt to lower his voice; he didn't care how many of them heard. "Goddamn you. Goddamn you forever."

Enoch's hands didn't tremble as they tied another knot.

TWENTY-ONE

Owen was wrong in thinking the news would break Molly. He remembered how big her eyes had been in an utterly still face, and he waited for her outcry against Enoch. It never came. She went on as though everything was unchanged. She had a tremendous inner strength. He never saw her weep, though in the mornings marks of weeping were on her face. The thing he couldn't understand about it all was that her feelings for Enoch seemed unchanged.

Owen stood at the window, thinking about what he was going to do. If it weren't for Molly, he would have left the ranch before now. She had never asked him to stay in so many words, but there was a pleading in her eyes, whenever she looked at him. If only she would talk to him about it, if only he could understand her thinking. But to all his insistence she would say, "It's done, Owen. Nothing can undo it."

Chad was out there in a snowbank with Scotty. Owen would lie awake at nights thinking about it. And the hating against Enoch made his muscles ache with cramping.

He thought gloomily, I shouldn't have stayed. But if he had gone, he was sure the E-P would go to hell. Not that that would have caused him any tears, but there was Molly to think about.

He knew Les and Abel and Hamp moved like they were walking on eggs, when they were around Enoch. His staying might have anchored them. I'll stay until spring, he thought. No longer.

Last night had brought fresh snow, but it had been a weak storm. Less than two inches had fallen. Winter was like a beaten man, throwing one last feeble punch. It should be ending, he thought. The chinook was already a month late.

Molly came and stood beside him. She looked out the window, and he worried about her thoughts.

She said, "He won't be back again until after dark."

Owen knew a flashing anger at her. She was concerned about Enoch. He could lay out in the snow and freeze, and Owen wouldn't lift a finger to save him. Enoch wasn't freezing. He was in town, getting drunk again. For the past two weeks, he had been gone every day, coming home late at night, mumbling to himself in his drunkenness. Owen thought bitterly: there wasn't enough whiskey in the world to drown the thoughts Enoch lived with.

Molly said, "He's got that bad cough, and—" Her words faded before the anger in his eyes. She said defensively, "Both of you are away so much now. I can't help but worry."

She couldn't be comparing his absence with Enoch's. Enoch was hiding, hiding from his own thoughts. Owen was seeking, looking for Linus Derks. He had watched the cabin on McDonald creek, and Linus hadn't returned to it. He had searched in town and found nothing. Maybe Linus was far out of the country and still running, but Owen didn't think so.

She placed her hand on his arm. "Bring him back, Owen. Please."

He stared at her in heavy silence. She didn't need him. All this time he had been fooling himself. She wanted Enoch, and he wanted to rage at her for it.

"Please," she repeated.

He nodded abruptly. He would do this one last thing for her. He would bring Enoch back, then he was free to leave. He didn't look at her as he put on his mackinaw.

Hamp came out into the corral as he was saddling his horse. He asked, "You need any of us?"

Owen shook his head. The following silence was uncomfortable. Hamp had something to say, and he didn't know how to say it.

"Owen," he said awkwardly. "This is bad."

"What's bad?" Owen asked curtly.

"All this hating," Hamp blurted. "It'll eat a man up. We've talked about it. Maybe there wasn't any other road for Enoch to take."

Owen glared at him. He had been giving himself undue credit. He wasn't holding the E-P together. The old loyalty to Enoch still remained.

He said harshly, "Mind your own business, Hamp."

"Sure," Hamp said stiffly and withdrew.

He left his horse at Hoyt's. He didn't have to ask if Enoch was in town. Enoch's horse was in the front stall. Hoyt wanted to talk, and Owen cut him off with a grim nod. He knew where to look for Enoch—in one of the saloons.

He passed Kilmonte's office as he moved down the street. He wasn't a half-dozen steps beyond the door, when Kilmonte called to him. He thought of ignoring the call, then he turned slowly.

"Come in, Owen. Just for a minute." That was almost begging in Kilmonte's tone.

He said, "We got nothing to talk about." He had tried to talk to Kilmonte, after the hanging. He had told him that he knew Linus Derks had been in that cabin.

Kilmonte had asked, "Did you see him?" At Owen's negative gesture, he said wearily, "You got no proof. None of them named him, did they?"

Owen had been tempted to lie, but Kilmonte knew differently. Kilmonte had talked to McLaughlin and Denton. Owen had said furiously, "I don't have to have my face rubbed in snow to know it's wet. You won't do anything?"

"I can't," Kilmonte replied.

That conversation was in Kilmonte's eyes as he studied Owen. Owen had said, "If I find Derks, I'll kill him." Kilmonte thought the determination hadn't weakened. He didn't want it happening. Molly Parnell had had enough grief. He didn't want to be the one to arrest Owen for murder.

Kilmonte said, "Enoch's in town. I want you to take him home."

"You ordering me to take him home?"

Kilmonte said wearily, "You know I'm not." He said with a quick rage, "You want to bring more grief to Molly?"

Owen said softly, "You can't mind your own business, can you, John?"

Kilmonte knew he couldn't reach Owen, but he still tried. With both Enoch and Owen looking for Linus Derks, one of them was bound to find him. He said, "Get Enoch out of town before I have to arrest him for killing Derks."

Owen's laugh was harsh. Kilmonte thought Enoch came to town looking for Linus. He didn't know Enoch was trying to drown himself in a sea of whiskey.

"All right, Owen," Kilmonte said. "I've done all I can."

He watched Owen move away. A man saw things forming, and he was powerless to change them. He wondered if Derks were still in town. He had seen him a week ago and repeated his warning to get out of town. He hoped Derks had sense enough to take the warning. Derks came to him right after it happened, squalling for protection.

Kilmonte had asked him, "What makes you think you need protection."

"They'll kill me," Derks had said shrilly. "You know how they are. The law's got to protect me."

Linus Derks was guilty as hell, Kilmonte thought. But no one could prove it. The law did have to protect him. All Kilmonte could do was to try to keep Owen and Enoch from finding him. The strain of the effort was graveling his disposition.

Linus Derks sprawled on Letty's bed. The whiskey bottle on the floor was empty. He hoped Letty would remember to bring him another one. It was hell being cooped up in this room, afraid to stick his head outdoors. He cursed Kilmonte for not doing something to stop the Parnells. A man should have some rights. If Kilmonte was worrying about his own life, things would be different.

He forgot the bottle was empty and reached for it. He flung it across the room in a sudden excess of rage.

He still trembled when he remembered how narrow his escape from that cabin had been. He had followed Chad out the rear door, stepping in Chad's boot prints. He had let Chad go on and cowered behind a big rock. Owen had stopped not three feet from him, and Linus was sure he was discovered. He was ready to shoot Owen, when Owen moved on, following Chad's tracks.

Kilmonte was always talking about the law. It was just talk and nothing more. Enoch Parnell had hanged four men. Did

Kilmonte arrest them? No! He cursed Kilmonte until his voice weakened. Kilmonte hadn't arrested anyone. Instead, he had warned Linus to get out of town.

He rubbed the back of his hand across his nose. What kind of protection was that? He had no doubt that either Enoch or Owen would shoot him on sight. Maybe that was what Kilmonte wanted.

Linus missed Cully. Things were going to be hard for him from now on. He had heard that Enoch left Cully out there. That was an awful thing, leaving a man out in that snow. He was going to do something about it, just as soon as he could. But a man couldn't do anything when he was forced to hide. He thought about Enoch, and he could taste the sickness of his hating. What kind of a man would hang his own son? And the law didn't touch him. Kilmonte should have arrested Enoch and everyone who was with him.

He stiffened as he heard a key turning in the lock. That should be Letty, but a man couldn't be positive. The strain left his face as she came into the room, and his eyes gleamed. She had the bottle of whiskey.

Her face grew furious, and he thought she was going to throw the bottle at him. "Get off my bed," she screamed. She looked around the room, and anger mottled her face. "Look at this room. It looks like a pigpen."

He stood and took the bottle from her. She was always complaining about something. The room looked all right to him. It didn't look any worse than when he first saw it.

He uncorked the bottle and took a long pull. Ah, that was better. The whiskey strengthened his will. The Parnells weren't going to run him away from his place. He had been comfortable there. He was going back to it. Maybe not right now, but in a few weeks.

He asked, "Anything happening?"

Her face was sullen. She couldn't stand him in this room much longer. He was out of money. She had seen him search his pockets for enough money to buy the bottle he held. He wasn't going to live off her.

She said, "Owen Parnell is in town."

Linus flinched. "He'd better stay away from me."

She said maliciously, "He thinks I know where you are. He told me he'll kill you on sight."

Linus said wildly, "You didn't—"

"I told him you were here." She put all the malice she could into the lie. She wanted him to sweat. As far back as she could remember she had hated this man. Chad was gone, and Cully was gone. She felt a deep self-pity. The last two times Chad had been to town, they had known a little happiness together. And now it was over. She was suddenly frightened at a glimpse of the years ahead of her, the lonely years. It was all Linus's fault

His face was frozen with shock, then he shuddered and drank from the bottle. He had to get to Kilmonte. Kilmonte had to protect him.

By the look on his face she knew she had a knife in him, and she twisted it. "He'll be coming here to see for himself"

Rage swept through Linus. It was hard to believe a man's own daughter would want to see him dead. He said, "Why damn you." He strode toward her and slashed her across the face with the back of his hand.

The blow knocked her onto the bed. She stared at him wide-eyed, a hand pressed against the sting. He was drunker than she realized, and hatred and fear of him warred within her For a moment, the fear she had pushed him too far was uppermost, but she couldn't back down. He wouldn't believe her, if she said she'd lied.

He moved toward her, his hand upraised. She sat up and tried to keep the trembling out of her voice. "Stay here. Stay here until he finds you. He followed me out of Schober's."

That stopped him. He put a frantic glance on the door, then cursed her in a thick voice. He couldn't stay here and be trapped in this room.

He ran to the wall and took down his mackinaw from its peg. He pulled his gun from its holster and held it in his hand. He took another long drink, and when he set the bottle down it was over half empty. The whiskey fought against the soft mass of fear inside him. If he could get to Kilmonte, he would be all right.

He moved to the door and eased it open. The hallway was empty. He turned his head and put a black look on her. She deserved killing for what she had done.

He stepped out into the hallway and looked down the stairs. They were empty. Should he wait here until Owen started up those stairs? The light wasn't too good, and he could miss If he missed, it left him with no retreat, except Letty's room.

He heard the door close behind him and the key turn in the

lock. He whirled and sprang toward it, intending to batter it down.

He stopped before he touched the door. He couldn't create a disturbance, he couldn't pull attention to him. He would deal with her later.

He moved down the steps, pistol in hand. His heart contracted at every squeak of the boards. He breathed more freely as he stepped outside and looked in both directions. No one was in sight. He shivered and buttoned his mackinaw. It was almost dark, and the wind had teeth in it. But the coming darkness and cold were working for him. No one would be out unless they had to.

He put hand and gun in his mackinaw pocket and turned toward Kilmonte's office. He had a block and a half to go. He could make it.

He stopped at the intersection and looked in every direction. The streets were deserted. He considered blackly that Letty was lying to him, that Owen wasn't even in town. He was tempted to go back and beat the lie out of her. He was turning it over in his mind, when he saw a figure turn the corner a block away. The gathering gloom left him unsure, but it could be Owen Parnell. He broke into a run across the intersection. Kilmonte's office was only a half block away.

He was panting, when he reached Kilmonte's office. But the fear was receding. Owen couldn't walk in here and shoot him. He tried the door, and it was locked. He refused to believe it, and he kept twisting at the knob. He didn't realize he was whimpering.

He cursed Kilmonte and he cursed Letty. Everybody locked their doors against him. The wild weakness passed, and he sorted out his prospects. Kilmonte had probably gone to supper. Linus could look for him in a restaurant, or he could wait here. He discarded both possibilities. He could walk into Owen, or Owen could see him standing here.

He needed a horse. If he had a horse, he could get out of town. He would steal the first one he saw. But few people were in town, and the tie racks were empty. No one left their horses out in cold like this.

The livery stable! His face brightened. He had no money, but he had a gun. He would take a horse from Hoyt.

He broke into a run, then checked himself after twenty yards. A running man commanded attention. He would have to move slowly and use the shadows.

He was regaining confidence as he approached the livery stable. That figure, he had seen, couldn't have been Owen. Imagination played fearful tricks on a man. Once he got a horse, he would be all right. He had some money buried. It would carry him a long way. A man was a fool anyway to stay in this damned, frozen country.

He turned the corner and froze. Two men stood in front of the livery stable. He was close enough to hear their voices. He pulled back around the corner and pressed against a wall. He heard Hoyt ask, "You want me to feed him, Owen," and Owen's curt refusal.

Linus's heart resumed its painful action. He was certain Owen would watch the stable. That escape was cut off to him. Now he had to find Kilmonte.

He pushed off the wall and went down the street. Fear was melting the bones in his legs. He wished he had brought that bottle with him. Good God, how he needed a drink.

He peered into Schober's restaurant and into Alma's café. Kilmonte wasn't in either of them. His fear was tearing him apart. It wasn't right for a man to feel like a trapped animal, to have to slink about for his life.

Hope that Kilmonte had returned to his office buoyed him, and he turned to retrace his steps. He hated the washes of light coming from the buildings along the street. He had to detour them or scurry quickly through them.

As he approached Springman's the door opened, and two men stepped out onto the walk. He shrank back into the shadows, then recognized them.

"Benton. Dougan," he said in a low voice. "Over here."

They turned their heads but didn't move. He said sharply, "You fools. Get out of that light."

They came toward him, their movements suspicious. Benton said, "It's you."

Linus caught the hostility in his voice. Dougan probably felt the same way. They blamed him for the loss of a brother and son.

He said, "Owen Parnell is in town. He's looking for us." At the last moment, he changed the "me" to "us." Let them sweat, too.

They exchanged startled glances. "Enoch's in Springman's," Dougan said.

The plan burst full-formed in Linus's head. He had been thinking of asking them to get him a horse, but he didn't have to run. He didn't have to leave his place. If he could pull them into

175

this, it would change the odds. The three of them against Enoch and Owen. And Kilmonte couldn't do a thing about it. A man had a right to save his life.

He said, "They're looking for us. I thought Owen had me a couple of blocks back."

Whiskey sharpened his mind. He prided himself on it. But it dulled other men's thinking. He would say by the heavy looks on their faces that they had taken on quite a load. They were turning his words over in their minds, and it looked as though they were laboring. Enoch and Owen were both in town. Owen would come to Springman's, looking for his father, and Linus could get the two of them.

"You're crazy," Dougan said. "The Parnells aren't looking for us."

Linus said gravely, "They are. Owen shot at me just a few minutes ago. They want all three of us."

Benton said heavily. "No. I've done nothing to them." His face twisted with a savage memory, and he cried, "My God. Haven't they done enough to me already?"

Linus leaned toward them. "Those boys weren't horse thieves." He nodded solemnly. "I know."

He had their attention. He waited until Dougan asked, "How do you know?"

"I was at that woodyard earlier in the day. Those boys just stumbled into the cabin to get warm. The horses were in the corral, when the boys got there. Somebody else put them there."

Benton stared at him. "What reason?"

Linus's voice was scornful. "Any fool could see it. The Parnells hid those horses out there, so they could accuse us of stealing them. The boys, happening on that cabin, made it easier for them."

Dougan swore, and the slackness left Benton's face. "Why did they do it?" Benton asked.

Linus sighed. The sigh said he had to point out every step to them. "They want our places. What happened at the woodyard gives them an excuse to move against us."

Benton gripped his arm. "Why weren't you there?"

"I wish to God I'd have stayed," Linus said. "I might've been able to stop it. I thought something was wrong with the setup. I told the boys to get out of there. They didn't listen to me."

Dougan was trying to seize an evasive thought. "Why haven't they moved at us before?"

Linus shrugged. "Who knows? Maybe they were afraid of the uproar they'd stirred up. Maybe they're waiting for it to die down. They're ready to move now. I told you they almost got me." His face was earnest. "I just wanted to warn you. I didn't want you shot down like dogs." He turned to leave, and Benton said, "Wait. Why didn't you go to Kilmonte with this?"

Linus said patiently, "Don't you think I did? He wouldn't listen to me." He tensed and peered down the block.

Dougan's voice shook as he asked, "What is it?"

"I guess I'm jumpy," Linus muttered. "I thought I saw Owen."

Dougan looked at Benton. "We'd better get our horses and leave."

Linus nodded. "Of course, if they miss you in town, they'll come to your places. They'd rather get you alone, anyway."

Dougan's voice went high-pitched. "Linus, what are we going to do?"

Linus said savagely, "Goddamn them. They kill our folks, and we run like rabbits. I'm tired of running. I'd like to make a stand of it."

He saw them exchange scared glances.

Benton asked in a small voice, "You mean walk up and call them."

"They don't deserve a fair fight. I say shoot them any way we can. The whole town knows they're looking for us."

Dougan said excitedly, "I'm for that. You got any ideas, Linus?"

Linus gave it some thought. "I'm scared," he confessed. "But I'm tired of running, too. And I want my place." He tapped his teeth and muttered, while they fidgeted.

His face brightened. "It might work. I'd be taking the big risk, but it's worth it to me." He would be taking a risk, but there was an element of risk in everything a man did. He was trusting that Enoch and Owen would follow a normal human impulse, that they would talk first. He would only need to keep them from action for a second or two. If he could work it out the way he wanted, Kilmonte couldn't say he had ambushed the Parnells. Kilmonte couldn't do a damned thing.

He said, "Owen will be going into Springman's, looking for Enoch. We'll be ready for them, when they come out. Dougan, if you get up on Springman's roof and Benton on Alderson's roof across the street, we could catch them in a cross fire. I'll stop them in the middle of the street." He said fiercely to hide his nervousness, "You shoot straight, you hear me?"

Benton said soberly, "You've got guts, Linus. Just give us our chance at them."

Linus said, "We may have quite a wait."

Dougan's voice was terse. "We'll wait."

Linus watched them move away. He was scared and excited. He would have his gun ready in his pocket. Enoch and Owen would have to dig under their coats for theirs. Linus would have the edge. He shouldn't need that edge—not with Benton and Dougan on opposite roofs.

He walked across the street to Alderson's store. The building was dark, and he guessed Alderson closed early these winter evenings. The waiting was hard. A man grew lonely and cold, standing here all by himself. He went backwards and forwards over his plan. His throat grew tight at the thought of how many things could go wrong. But if it worked, he stood to gain a lot. Wasn't Letty Chad's widow? Wouldn't she have a claim on what the Parnells owned? His teeth bared. Wasn't that worth a lot of risk?

A tin roof extended over the walk, and above the roof was a wooden parapet, some three feet high. He was sure he heard the sound of crunching snow on Alderson's roof. That should be Benton, walking across the roof from the alley.

"Benton?" he asked in a hoarse whisper.

"Yes," Benton replied.

Linus could not see Dougan across the street, but he knew he was there.

"You think it will work?" Benton called down in a strained voice.

"It'll work," Linus said. Only the waiting remained—the fearful, tense waiting.

TWENTY-TWO

Springman's was the last saloon Owen tried. It was dark as he stepped inside, and the heat from the potbellied stove felt good. On the ride home, he would be wishing he had some of that heat with him.

Springman's face brightened as he saw Owen, and he jerked his head toward the end of the bar. Enoch stood there, or rather clung to the end of the bar. His head was down, and he muttered something. He looked bad; he looked old and broken. This was something new, Enoch drinking this heavily, and it worried Springman. Owen felt no pity for his father. Enoch had a right to his heavy drinking. It would take a lot of whiskey to drown the face that was haunting him.

He moved to Enoch and took his arm. "Molly wants you home," he said.

He hated to say that much to Enoch. He swore he would never speak to him again, unless absolute necessity demanded it. Maybe this was one of those times.

Resentment flared in Enoch's eyes. "You think I'm drunk, don't you?"

If he wasn't, he was giving a good imitation of it.

"I'm not," he said. Something else was on his mind, and the inability to say it tortured his eyes.

"You coming?" Owen asked harshly.

Enoch moved with him. Owen didn't look at Springman as he passed him.

At the door Enoch said, "Owen—" Again, there was that long, tortured pause.

Owen stared at him, and his eyes were merciless judges.

Enoch said it fast, as if he were afraid that the words would block in his mouth. "You stay away from him. He's mine."

"Stay away from who?" Owen snapped.

"Linus Derks."

Owen said cruelly, "Do you expect to find him, holding up a bar?" He saw the shudder run through Enoch. He had hurt him, and he felt no remorse.

He stepped outside, and Enoch followed him. Enoch slipped on a patch of ice. He would have fallen, if Owen's arm hadn't supported him. The help was instinctive with no personal feeling.

He said brusquely, "Are you coming?" and moved down the walk ahead of Enoch.

He hadn't gone a half-dozen steps when he saw a dark figure detach itself from Alderson's store and move to the middle of the street.

"Owen," Linus Derks bawled. "I want to talk to you." He stopped at the edge of light reaching out from Springman's window.

Owen turned toward him, feeling curiously detached. A warning jangled in his brains. Surely Derks knew Owen was looking for him. Yet Derks was sure of himself for some reason. Behind him, Owen heard Enoch ask querulously, "Who is it?"

Owen stopped four feet from Derks. "I've been looking for you," he said.

Derks unbuttoned and threw open his mackinaw. "I'm not armed, Owen. You can't shoot an unarmed man. I just want to talk."

The jangle of warning grew louder, honing Owen's alertness. Derks was bold, or drunk. Probably some of both, but what was the reason behind it.

Enoch stopped beside Owen, and peered at Derks. The whiskey was making recognition hard for him.

"Give me your gun, Enoch," Owen said. Derks wasn't leaving this spot.

Recognition rasped in Enoch's voice. "No, Goddamn it. He's mine."

Derks turned his head toward Alderson's store. Owen, watching his every move, saw the tilt of his head. Derks was looking toward the roof.

Owen saw a dark shape rise up beyond the parapet. "Down," he yelled and dove for the street.

If Enoch heard him, he didn't act on the warning. He tried to unbutton his coat and reach for his gun at the same time.

"Shoot," Linus Derks squalled and ran back a few steps.

Owen rolled after he hit the street. He cursed the coat's bulkiness as he tried to find his gun. A bullet plocked into the street beside his head, kicking snow into his face. He rolled again and got the gun free. He snapped a shot at the dark figure on Alderson's roof and heard the shrill, following scream. The figure broke at the waist and fell across the parapet. It hung there a long moment, then tumbled onto the tin roof over the walk. The roof clattered and sagged as the figure rolled across it. The body fell into the street. It fell limply like an abused rag doll.

Something heavy and hot tore through Owen's coat and burned across his shoulder. That shot came from the other side of the street, from Springman's roof, and he flung himself about. He caught a glimpse of movement up there and fired three rapid shots. The shadowy bulk disappeared, and he was sure he heard frantic footsteps retreating across the roof. He flopped over to face Derks. Derks had a gun in his hand, a gun aimed at Enoch.

Enoch got his gun out as Derks fired. An orange tongue of flame licked out at Enoch, and Owen heard the soft thud of bullet hitting flesh. Enoch grunted and staggered, and his steps broke backward. He didn't go down. Some stubborn determination kept him on his feet as he fought to aim his pistol. He grunted again as he was hit the second time. Derks was screaming at him. Laboriously, Enoch steadied his gun hand. He fired, and his aim was true. Derks uttered a coughing sigh and rose high on his toes. He bent slowly and started to fall. Owen fired at him in that moment, knowing the shot wasn't needed. Linus Derks was dead at the instant he started to fall.

Enoch sagged to one knee. His pistol had suddenly gone heavy, and he fought to raise his hand. The wracking struggle was etched on his face, pulling his lips back from his teeth. It was awful watching that tormented face trying to will strength into failing muscles.

Owen called, "No, Enoch. He's dead." He pushed to his feet.

His words reached Enoch, for he turned his face toward Owen, and some of the terrible strain eased from it. "Did I kill him?"

"Yes," Owen answered. Before he could cross the few feet to Enoch, Enoch said, "I'm glad." He let go and fell on his face.

Owen thought he was dead; then he heard the heavy, rasping breathing. He turned him over gently, and Enoch looked at him with glazing eyes. "He hit me pretty hard," he said.

Owen looked around for help. Men were timidly moving out of their stores and homes, drawn by the shooting and not quite sure the danger was over.

Owen roared, "Get Rockwood. Quick."

He kneeled in the street, holding Enoch's upper body in his arms. He thought the first pounding footsteps he heard were the doctor's, but it was Kilmonte.

Enoch's eyes were closed, and Kilmonte didn't hear his breathing.

His face asked the question, and Owen shook his head. "No. But Derks is dead. There's another one in front of Alderson's. The third one was on Springman's roof. He ran."

He held Enoch and watched Kilmonte go first to Derks, then to the man in front of Alderson's. Wouldn't that damned doctor ever get here?

Kilmonte came back and said, "That's Benton." His face was hard with thought. "He and Dougan were together earlier. I'll pick up Dougan and see what part he had in it."

Owen said in a tired voice, "Linus had it set up pretty good. I wondered how he had enough guts to stop us."

Kilmonte nodded. "It's plain. You hurt, Owen?"

Owen felt the fierce burning in his shoulder, but he could move the arm. "No," he said impatiently. "Where's Rockwood?"

Kilmonte looked over the heads of the pushing ring of men. He said, "He's coming now." He roared at the crowd, "Stand back. Stand back. Let Rockwood through."

Rockwood came through the opened lane and kneeled beside Owen. "I'll take him," he said.

Rockwood eased Enoch onto the street and made a quick examination. He did not shake his head as he looked at Owen, but the negative gesture was back of his expression. "We'd better get him to my office as fast as we can."

Enoch opened his eyes. "No. Take me home."

Rockwood shook his head. "He can't be moved that far."

Enoch swore at him with surprising strength. "Owen. Take me home." The old command was in his voice.

Owen pulled Rockwood to one side. "How bad is he?"

Rockwood made it simple and brutal. "He's dying."

Owen thought so. If Enoch could make it, he had a right to die at home. He looked at Kilmonte and asked, "John will you get me a rig from the stable?"

"Sure," Kilmonte said gruffly and ran down the street.

"He'll never make the trip," Rockwood said.

"Fix him up as well as you can," Owen ordered. Enoch would make the trip. That stubborn spark in him would see that he did.

Kilmonte came back with the rig and helped Owen lift Enoch into the rear seat. He took a horse blanket from the seat and tucked it about Enoch. He asked, "Need me?"

Owen shook his head. He said, "Thanks, John."

Kilmonte bobbed his head, and there was embarrassment in the gesture.

Owen looked at Derks. The crowd was gathered about the rig. Derks lay by himself. Not quite by himself, for a woman kneeled beside him.

Owen walked to her. Letty looked up at his approach. Her face was blank, and her voice had no feeling as she said, "He's dead."

"Yes," Owen said. He could find no sympathy for her.

Her face twisted with some rush of feeling. "What am I going to do?" she cried. "What's going to happen to me?"

Owen looked at her. "You'll find a way to make out." He turned and walked back to the rig.

It was a hellish trip home. Enoch never lost consciousness, and it would have been better if he had. Owen drove as fast as he dared. Those jolts must have been tearing Enoch apart, but only three or four groans escaped him.

Owen was yelling at the top of his lungs as he drove into the yard. Hamp and Abel and Les ran out from the bunkhouse, and Owen said, "It's Enoch. Help me get him into the house."

The kitchen door opened, and Molly was framed in the oblong of light. Owen went to her. "Enoch's hurt bad," he said. "Linus Derks is dead."

Her face went white and still, but he saw the way her hands clenched. When she spoke, her voice was low but steady. "I'll get the bed ready."

He went back to help with Enoch, and they carried him into the house. His face looked ghastly in the light, and Owen thought, I didn't make it.

Enoch opened his eyes and looked at her. He said, "Molly."

She touched his cheek. "Yes, Enoch."

Owen thought wonderingly, he had to make it, if only for this much.

Molly said crisply, "Bring him in here."

They laid him on the bed and stood awkwardly around. "I can manage now," Molly said. "Owen, if you'll help me get his coat off."

Hamp said, "You'll call us, if—"

"Yes," Molly interrupted him. A growing impatience was in her voice.

They filed awkwardly out of the room, each man looking back at the door.

Owen removed Enoch's heavy coat. His shirt front was matted with blood. Stark fear was in Molly's eyes as she looked at Owen, but strength remained in her voice. "Bring me some hot water, Owen."

She met him at the door and took the pan from his hands. She closed the door gently in his face.

Owen spent the rest of the long night, wandering about the kitchen. When he went to the bedroom door and tapped lightly, Molly would open it, shake her head, then close the door.

She refused breakfast, and Owen saw the increasing strain pulling at her. Her helplessness to do anything showed in her eyes, but she would not let Owen share that helplessness.

He stood outside that door and listened to the hoarse, labored breathing. He heard Molly talking to Enoch in a little, crooning voice she would have used to a child. He thought with helpless rage: Oh God. End it. You're tearing her apart.

Enoch fought dying as hard as he fought living. It was well into the second night before Molly came into the kitchen and said, "He wants to see you." Her eyes and voice were dead.

Owen walked into the bedroom and looked at a dead man on the bed. Yet there was a fluttering in the eyelids and a tiny movement of the nostrils.

Enoch opened his eyes and looked up at Owen. "Owen," he said and stopped. Some terrible entreaty was in those eyes, a reaching out that he wanted to put into words. "Owen." He tried again. The words would not come. He sighed, and the light went out in his eyes.

Owen stood there a long moment staring at his father. The rending hurt inside him threatened to tear him apart, and he could find no relief for it. His eyes remained dry. How could you find tears for a man you didn't love?

He turned and walked back into the kitchen. He said harshly, "He didn't say anything to me."

Molly said almost absently, "I didn't think he could."

TWENTY-THREE

It was mid-March before the flat pancake chinook clouds appeared above the mountains. Owen dismounted and stripped the saddle from his horse. There was no thawing yet, but he thought it would start tomorrow. The air and the earth had a different feel, as if there were a stirring of life in both. He did not look at the snowbank behind the barn. Scotty and Chad and Enoch were there, waiting for burial. All of them were claimed one way or another by this country, and Owen cursed Montana with a savage rush of feeling.

He shouldered his saddle and carried it to the rack. When he came out of the barn, Hamp and Les and Abel were coming in. He waited for their reports. Their reluctance to speak told him how bad it was. They had found the same thing he had.

Les spoke first. He sighed and said, "Owen, I don't think a head of those Texas cattle came through. We looked at cow carcasses all day long. When the thaw comes, a man won't be able to get near some of the valleys and coulees for the smell."

Everybody was reporting the same. On Owen's last trip to town, he had talked to McLaughlin and Denton and both had reported staggering losses. Some people said Montana had lost sixty per cent of her cattle. They quoted wild figures like three hundred and sixty thousand head dead. It was a figure too big for a man's mind to absorb.

Hamp said, "I figure about thirty per cent of our original herd pulled through, Owen."

Owen said passionately, "I'll never own another animal I can't give feed and shelter to."

They stared at him in embarrassment, then drifted away.

Owen turned and walked to the kitchen. He stepped inside, and Molly was just taking off her coat and hat.

"I just beat you home," she said. A ghost of a smile played about her lips. "I've been cooped up in this house too long."

He was happy to see the change in her. It was as though she was stepping from holding shadows. He had worried about her after Enoch's death. He never saw tears in her eyes, but the evidence of them was there after the lonely, night hours.

He said, "Maw, we're hurt bad."

"Not too bad," she said briskly. "You never have too little left to start again."

He walked to the window and stared out it. He thought irritably, she doesn't know had bad it is. Here and there, a patch of earth was beginning to show. It was the first bare ground he had seen in weeks. He heard the drip of water from the eaves. The thaw was starting.

He cursed Montana with a bitter intensity. The thaw would go on all night, and little snow would remain in the morning. But it came too late, more than a month too late. Spring would lay its false promise over the land. The first faint flush of green would deepen into a thick cloak, and a man would hope that the coming year would be a better one. Spring was a lying jade.

She moved to the window and stood beside him. She said, "How often I've heard him curse the land like you did."

He frowned at her. "Who?"

"Enoch," she said simply. Some memory moved her lips in a tender smile.

It looked like a good memory, and it angered him. How could anyone have feeling for a man who had no feeling?

He said harshly, "He didn't care for anybody in his life."

"You're wrong, Owen. He loved you and Chad. And me."

He wanted to shock her out of this nonsense. "He showed it," he said brutally.

Her face remained calm. "You're thinking of Chad. For a little while, I felt as you do. But don't you see, Owen? It wasn't the Chad we knew at all. That Chad was gone. What was done had to be done. I've thought about it for a long time. I think Enoch was the only man I ever knew who could have done it."

He said incredulously, "You're proud of him for it?"

She shook her head. "Not proud. Oh, God, not proud. But not holding it against him because he saw what had to be done."

"No," he said stubbornly. This was the first time they had talked about it, and he felt it would be the only time. He wanted to understand her thinking.

"Would you have let Chad go free?" she asked. She saw the indecision in his face. "Then the others had to go free, too. And Enoch would never have killed Linus Derks. Everybody but you can see it. Have you heard Les or Abel or Hamp blaming Enoch? Or anybody in town? He was strong enough to forget a name."

Owen stared at the floor. What she said about everybody not blaming Enoch was true. Kilmonte had tried to talk to Owen about it, and his words had been awkward. A man lived or died by the laws of his country.

She said, "You never really knew him, Owen. He was afraid to show sentiment. He buried it deep. I think I was the only person who did know him."

Owen lifted his head. "I knew all I wanted to know of him."

She shook her head, but there was understanding in the gesture. "You didn't know him at all. You saw only the surface. You saw only the things he had to do."

The stubbornness remained on his face, and she said, "You thought he didn't care about Chad. I've heard him cry, when he didn't know I was awake. I think he started dying the moment it happened."

He stared at her with troubled eyes. It was all wrong, and she could stand here, calmly explaining it.

"He walked a lonely road, Owen. He was hard and unwavering in his determination. He had to be. This is a savage country. It took men like Enoch to shape something out of it. He tried to give you the one thing he could. He tried to fit you and Chad to live here, too. Chad couldn't make it."

Owen was silent. Maybe someday he would know a respect for his father. But not now, he thought. Not now.

Molly smiled. "You're a lot like him, Owen."

He stared at her in outrage. "No," he said explosively.

She nodded. "The same stubbornness. The same determination. Maybe not as hard. I'm glad for that. Maybe men like Enoch civilized this country so that men following them don't have to be so hard. He talked about you before he died. More than I have ever heard him talk. He said you were right, and he was wrong. He was proud of you. Almost the last thing he said to me was. 'Molly, he'll build better than I ever did.'"

She touched his arm. "He built and left all this for you, Owen. Do you want it?"

Did he want it? He turned the question over in his mind. Wherever he rode on this range, ghosts would ride beside him— Chad and Scotty and Enoch. And they left him standards, standards against which he would always be measuring himself.

This evening, it seemed too big a job. This evening, he didn't want it.

He started to speak, when he saw a rider approaching. He turned a strained face toward Molly.

"It's Evlalie," he said and flight was in his expression.

Molly's face was serene. "I was afraid she had weakened. I rode over to see her this afternoon. I told her if she wanted you, she'd better get over here. Women understand talk like that."

He wanted to yell at her meddling. He said, "She made her choice."

"Did you ask her?"

"I've got eyes," he growled.

"You didn't give her much chance, did you? A woman can't speak first. She has to wait for her man to do it. When he doesn't, she has to try to make him."

He glanced out of the window. Evlalie was riding into the yard. In a moment, she would be walking into the kitchen. He didn't want to see her—not after everything that had happened.

Molly said scornfully, "You can hide in your room. I'll tell her you're gone."

He scowled at her, and she said in exasperation, "I want this empty house filled. You still love her, don't you?"

"I never quit."

"Then tell her so." She crossed the kitchen to the inner door and closed it behind her.

He wanted to call her back. He didn't want to talk to Evlalie alone.

He opened the door before she knocked. His face was wooden. "Hello, Evlalie."

He stood in the doorway, and she asked, "Aren't you going to ask me in?"

He stepped aside and followed her into the room. He had a thousand things on his mind to say, and none of them would come to his tongue.

She pulled off her gloves and said, "It's melting outside."

He blurted out the question that was uppermost in his mind. He didn't mean to say it. It just popped out. "Where's Sawtelle?"

She said angrily, "Am I supposed to know?"

They stared at each other like two strange species. "You knew, last summer," he said.

Color was high in her cheeks. "What was I supposed to do? Sit around, while you talked to Tom? You never paid me any attention. It was flattering to have Clell's."

He said accusingly, "You brought him along when you came to see me after I was hurt."

"He joined me on the way over. He was trying to pay you a neighborly call. Should I have told him not to come?" She ducked her head, and he had the thought she was doing it to hide the tears springing into her eyes. "After Chad and Letty left here, people said it was because you and Chad fought over her."

"You believed that?"

She looked at him. He was right about the tears. "The way you acted around her at the dance. Then you wouldn't see me. What else could I think?" She shook her head in angry negation at herself. "I wish I hadn't promised Molly I would come. She said you and I were wasting our lives. She was wrong."

No, Molly wasn't wrong. Evlalie was here, and what more proof did he want? He seized her shoulders. She tried to push him away with a half-hearted effort.

"Evlalie, could you love a fool?"

She tried to resist as he raised her face. Then the resistance was gone, and she gave him her lips. The old, sweet promise was there, and he knew with a quick certainty it would never dim.

She clung to him half crying and half laughing. "Owen," she said. "Don't ever shut me out again."

"No," he said fervently. A man needed three things to make his life whole—his work, his home, and his woman. And he had all of them right here.

His arm tightened about her as they looked out the window. In the gathering darkness, the land looked softer. It was only an illusion, and a man must never be fooled by it. He listened to the dripping of the water. There were bad days ahead, hard days of rebuilding. But a determined man could top those days. He thought, that determination had to be bred in a man. He could think of Enoch with no bitterness.

"Evlalie," he said soberly. "I wouldn't want to be anyplace else."

ZANE GREY'S
GREAT
WESTERNS

_____ 80451 ARIZONA AMES $1.50

_____ 81434 BOULDER DAM $1.50

_____ 81326 FORLORN RIVER $1.50

_____ 81017 KNIGHTS OF THE RANGE $1.50

_____ 81136 LIGHT OF WESTERN STARS $1.50

_____ 81321 LONE STAR RANGER $1.50

_____ 81325 LOST PUEBLO $1.50

_____ 81275 MAN OF THE FOREST $1.50

_____ 80454 MYSTERIOUS RIDER $1.50

_____ 80453 RAINBOW TRAIL $1.50

_____ 81374 ROBBERS' ROOST $1.50

Available at bookstores everywhere, or order direct from publisher.   ZGA

POCKET BOOKS
Department Z GA
1230 Avenue of the Americas
New York, N.Y. 10020

Please send me the books I have checked above. I am enclosing
$_____ (please add 50¢ to cover postage and handling). Send check
or money order—no cash or C.O.D.'s please.

NAME _____

ADDRESS_____

CITY_____STATE/ZIP_____

ZGA